A Blissful Moment of Nothingness

Susanna Ho

Strategic Book Publishing and Rights Co.

Strategic Book Publishing and Rights Co., LLC
USA | Singapore
www.sbpra.net

For information about special discounts for bulk purchases, please contact Strategic Book Publishing and Rights Co. Special Sales, at bookorder@sbpra.net.

ISBN: 978-1-68235-612-8

Book Design: Suzanne Kelly

For the Freedom Fighters . . .
You are my heroes and heroines.
You are my hands and feet.

AUTHOR'S NOTE

I once held an impression that writing after the first book would be easy, but this project proved me wrong. It's been a long process, writing a story with a zigzag time sequence. When I started writing the story in January of 2013, I had no idea that it would last so long. After conceiving the plot within a few months, I thought it would be just another book project and didn't expect the story would mean so much to me. My protagonist's horoscope predicted the imminent changes in life. How true! Only when we look back can we see our lives more clearly.

In the years of writing this book, I carried on teaching in a university. No major events took place in my life except for a few personal losses and inconveniences. Due to a car accident, my father lost his mobility in 2014. In the same and following years, I lost four canine friends, one after another. However, my personal setbacks were no comparison to those experienced by many Hong Kong citizens since the Umbrella Movement in 2014. Frustrations and heartbreaking moments over the last few years made my story. Writing the novel was like sharing common sorrows with people whom I had not yet met in person. I then realised that writing is no longer a hobby or a pastime; I must write for others, and I must write for a bigger cause.

My hope was to publish this novel before June 2019, to commemorate two events—the thirtieth anniversary of the Tiananmen Square protests, and the centennial of William Butler Yeats's poem "Nineteen Hundred and Nineteen." When I didn't manage to publish my book then, my disappointment soon turned into great revelation—I cannot complete my story without writing about the Hong Kong people's resistance against the government's proposal of passing an extradition law, ignoring the peaceful marches on the ninth and the sixteenth of June in 2019 with historic turnouts of 1.03 million, and two million protesters on two consecutive Sundays. So much had happened, both good and bad, in the last few months. I saw bravery and self-sacrifice on the part of the protesters as much as violence and excessive force exercised by those in power. I then understood that commemorating two anniversaries aside, I had to tell an ongoing story about the city where I lived most of my life.

Let me dedicate my story to those who love Hong Kong, a truly amazing city that so many of us call home, whether permanent or temporary. Anyone who's lived here would agree with me that the place has a lot to offer. It is a vibrant city; one never gets bored with it. But like a living organism that grows old, a city also experiences stagnation. To keep Hong Kong young and lively, and to keep it going, it needs nourishment to regain its strength and find a new existence. I hope my book is one of the sources.

Keeping me writing are my family and a circle of close friends who have been patiently waiting for my writing and my thoughts to mature. Whether my writing has become better is not for me to judge, but oftentimes it takes me deep and long reflections to formulate an idea. Special thanks go to Brian and Simmie, my Canadian friends who spent time filling me in with the geography of Winnipeg, a place of importance in this novel.

September 2019, Hong Kong

TABLE OF CONTENTS

But is there any comfort to be found?
Man is in love and loves what vanishes,
What more is there to say?

—William Butler Yeats,
"Nineteen Hundred and Nineteen"

PART I
MARCH 2013
HONG KONG

SNAPSHOTS

It all began with the rain. The morning sky was blanketed with thick, dark clouds, making it a perfect day to stay home indulging in the little pleasures in life. Staying in a sunless apartment would have been depressing for anyone not well-prepared. It would, however, be uplifting to sit at the breakfast table sipping tea, spreading fruit jam on toast, and sinking her teeth into fat, juicy plums in slow motion, without the trouble of switching the light on as one would normally do in a room that fell into darkness after sunset. It was not necessary to make that special effort, for the apartment was already quite dark. It required artificial lighting right from the start.

Margaret's Sunday paper arrived punctually. Flipping through the main news at the rhythm of the patter of rain on the window, she saw nothing of her interest, so she turned to the back page, munching over her horoscope, slowly digesting the reading:

> *What's going to happen next week is rather unsettling. You may not be able to make sense of all these changes now. Only when you look back one day will you then realise that there is a good reason behind them. Don't expect life to be simple. It is not, and anyway, you wouldn't have appreciated it if it had been so.*

She would usually ignore the so-called prediction. Either it was too vague to shed any light, or it was too absurd to be true. But this one was different. What could it mean? She read it once, twice, and was compelled to read it again later at noon. Her feeling of boredom was short-lived and disturbed by this intriguing horoscope reading.

For the rest of the day, she racked her brain trying to work out its meaning. The thought was so overwhelming that she couldn't sleep. Tossing and turning in bed, she wondered why. *Nothing much happened, so why can't I go to sleep*, she thought with a sigh. Sleep would come soon, she assured herself. This brought disquiet rather than solace.

She finally lost patience and stopped forcing herself to try to go to sleep. Instead, she let the happenings of the day run through her mind again. What was supposed to be an uneventful Sunday unexpectedly marked a new beginning. The rain made her stay home and gave her time to do housework. She even had the luxury of looking at some old photos that had been stored, untouched, for ages. The sudden appearance of all the long-forgotten faces had inevitably created a very bizarre impression.

Still lying in bed, it became clear to Margaret that it was the photos that did the trick to her mind. Again, nobody knew what triggered her to look at them on that Sunday. But all the same, the chain of events that took place the following week were so out of the ordinary that she could never have imagined them. So much happened in the following week, both in her routine and in her mind, that she had to refer to the reading again.

Margaret was used to leading an unsettled life. She grew up in Hong Kong and moved to Canada, her mother's home country, when she was fifteen. It was her mother, Betty, who made the decision when she saw tanks moving in the direction of the Tiananmen Square on TV. She was very much distressed and wouldn't agree to stay in the city for any longer than she had to, even though she was married to a native Chinese. Margaret didn't understand what her mother was afraid of. Didn't her father have close business allies whom he could seek help from in Mainland China?

After Margaret moved to Canada with her family, she did go back and visit her friends in Hong Kong, but she didn't move back to reside in the city until she turned thirty, the year when she experienced a major setback in life. Having divorced her husband, who was a second-generation Canadian of Welsh origin, she was unfortunately left penniless and, rather fortunately, childless. After a month of self-pity came a sense of liberation. She lost count of the number of sleepless nights she spent with Carol, who tirelessly talked, cried, and laughed with her over Martinis, listening to her marriage saga. When the self-therapy was over, Margaret found a new strength and decided to free herself from any romantic relationships for a while.

Turning thirty is a big deal to many women, and Margaret was no exception. But the year seemed to make a much bigger impact. She had to think twice before she ticked the boxes in a form again. Marital status? *Single.* Place of residence? *Hong Kong*. Or so she thought.

Margaret knew that life wasn't easy, especially for someone like her who was always on the move. She couldn't remember how many countries she had resided in during her marriage. Every year or so, her ex-husband, Brent, would be assigned to a new project that took them to a new place. It was quite fun in the beginning, but when the job of flat hunting and relocation fell to her, she found the pattern repetitive and tiring.

The first thing Margaret wanted after her divorce was to have control over her life. In 2004, when Hong Kong's economy was still sluggish in the aftermath of SARS, Margaret saw her opportunity. The fact that nearly three hundred people died the year before did not discourage her business planning. It wasn't exactly a smooth ride; money was rather tight during the first three years. But an overseas education combined with a foreign look turned out to be her best bargaining power. Don't be mistaken that she did not work hard. Margaret put long hours and a lot of brainwork into her start-up that finally broke even in its fourth year. She worked as hard as, if not harder than, most people living in big cities: long hours, short lunch breaks, and an absence of pleasure trips. Any travelling Margaret did was work-related. After she moved back to Hong Kong, she only saw her parents twice: first in Beijing in 2008, then two years later in Canada. Margaret still remembered what a pain it was to arrange the second reunion. After endless negotiations over long-distance calls, she finally convinced her mother to fly two and a half hours to meet her in Vancouver.

"Can you not fly over to see us when you are done with your business?" asked Betty in a voice filled with great impatience.

"I would if I could, but I can't. I simply don't have the time," replied Margaret in an equally impatient tone. "What's keeping you? What's there to do in the winter? Aren't you happy to get away from the wind and the snow?"

"It snows everywhere in Canada." Betty quickly picked up on the illogical reasoning. "We usually stay indoors, so it doesn't really matter if the weather is horrible. Fly over to see us, so your father doesn't need to travel. You know how much he hates flying."

True, her father had made so many business trips between Hong Kong, China, and Canada that he preferred not to travel anymore now that he had retired. But Margaret also knew that her father wouldn't mind the trip as long as his beloved daughter awaited him on the other end. She only had her mother to work on.

"But it will at least be a little warmer in Vancouver. Hey, look, if you can talk Dad into it, I will pay for everything, literally everything."

"Including our taxi fares?"

Margaret managed to bite her tongue to refrain from saying anything that might provoke her mother. "Of course. Why not? The whole point is for the three of us to have some fun together. When was the last time we ate dim sum in Chinatown and did scenic drives?"

"Ever since you got married?"

Betty was right. Almost immediately after they got married, Margaret and Brent kept moving from one country to another until a permanent post was offered back in Winnipeg. Marrying Brent at the age of twenty-two was nothing but acting on impulse. Margaret was having her so-called gap year after graduating with a degree in philosophy, which she knew wouldn't land her a promising job unless she continued with her studies. But she wasn't academic.

Meeting Brent opened up a whole new experience. When most of her friends were from the university, meeting someone already well into his career was exciting. He took her to expensive restaurants that she didn't even know existed before. Most places she ever ate in were cafeterias in the university. Sometimes she ate in the Japanese restaurant where she worked part-time, and occasionally the one where Carol worked, or the one that served crepes in the downtown area. So, when she was shown the glamorous life, she couldn't resist being captured. It didn't take long to accept the proposal of marriage. How could she reject something that was done in style? But what started in style sadly ended in disaster. Margaret was once very upset about her unsuccessful marriage, but having got over it, she decided to become independent of anyone, including her father, whose shoulder she would cry on every time she failed at something.

Having freed herself from any emotional attachments, Margaret thought it best to do what people in Hong Kong are good at: simply working hard. She was, after all, a half-local. She was one of the lucky few whose diligence paid off. Over the years, she had accumulated a rather handsome amount in her bank account. When life became more stable, she even dared to decline appointments from clients on Sundays. She made it very clear that the day was reserved for personal indulgences such as sleeping in, having an elaborate and long breakfast, going for a spa and facial treatment, shopping, or doing nothing at all. While she was quite good at pampering herself, she tended to neglect the importance of keeping the spirit satisfied and fulfilled.

Tending her spiritual feelings was something that Margaret had never been very good at. Calling herself a city girl, she would rather spend time shopping for luxury goods and eating in expensive restaurants. She didn't want to miss out on anything that was considered hot and trendy. Nothing was more important than being in possession of expensive items that most people could only dream of. She was never shy of showing off her new acquisitions on the social networks.

Her show-off lists included expensive handbags, shoes, and newly acquired boyfriends, some of them cute and young, and others more mature (meaning old and boring) but filthy rich. In order to make her lists long and interesting, she spent time updating them. Anyone who regularly visited Margaret's page would be fascinated by the changes.

So, as a person rather careless with her feelings, that sleepless night was an onset of an emotional beginning. Margaret had an urge to track down her friends from the old days. It was amazing that she was still keeping their photos after years of living abroad. As someone who was usually not sentimental, especially not after her failed marriage, Margaret had no idea why she had this strong desire to see them again. This overwhelming emotion that she hadn't felt for so many years scared her.

Margaret couldn't stay in bed anymore. She put on her robe and went to the storeroom again. She placed the photos under the light so that she could see them clearly. Calling out her friends' names one by one, she reacted to her voice: *Cindy*, she said with a smile; *Tsz Ching* came with a frown; *Dominic*, she sighed a long sigh; and finally *Nathan*, when she remained silent and felt a tug on her heartstrings.

Stored with the photos was a piece of paper that had turned yellowish. Seeing the address again in her own handwriting, she remembered that summer. This old and almost forgotten item made her hands shake violently. Suddenly, her chest was enveloped with an excruciating pain; she collapsed and broke down into great sobs.

VIRTUAL REUNION

The first thing Margaret did the following morning was turn on her laptop. She was quite hopeful to be able to track down her friends, one way or another. As long as they used the internet, they would almost certainly leave some traces here and there, wouldn't they? To narrow down her search, she typed each of their names and the school they went to, thinking that it would be quite easy. But after a few attempts, she found nothing. To prove there was nothing wrong with this method, Margaret made a search for her own digital footprint. She did find her company website and her social pages, so the problem had to do with her friends. They either did not use the internet very often or they made an effort of erasing their traces.

What was she supposed to do now? If she was to succeed in this manhunt, she had to come up with a plan. First, she had to focus on fewer of them, make it a less ambitious project. She would begin with her classmate Cindy, whose smiling face was unforgettable, then Nathan, her first boyfriend, and finally, Dominic, her special friend, both of whom she met outside school.

The major difficulty of her search lay in the fact that she was not dealing with celebrities—not her friends anyway. So how was she supposed to find these nobodies on the internet? But surely her boyfriend wasn't completely unknown in the sports arena.

Most of what happened in that summer was a blur in Margaret's memory, but some parts had been securely stored and could be retrieved if she wanted to. Margaret was now holding a photo in her hand, the only thing left of her boyfriend. All the cards and letters he sent her were destroyed. Nineteen eighty-nine was a good year for him; he won many prizes and trophies, both in Hong Kong and the Asia-Pacific region. With the backdrop of a swimming pool, he was holding his gold medal, smiling at the spectators. On the back of the photo was scribbled "Love, Nathan" in his neat handwriting.

Margaret decided that she had to stop looking at the photo and continue with her search. She typed his full name and "front crawl." So many results popped up on the screen that she couldn't believe her eyes. By the time she finished reading all the websites, she found out that not only did he keep winning competitions in both local and overseas events in the early 1990s, he had also set a record in Hong Kong that nobody had yet broken. One of the photos available on the internet showed a confident young man beaming with great pleasure. He looked so content with life that he seemed to be telling everyone that the world was his oyster; all he had to do was give it a go. Wondering whether his dream had come true, Margaret was suddenly overcome with a burning desire to see him again.

Margaret then reasoned with herself that if he had made a name in Hong Kong, he had to be somebody whom his fellow schoolmates would look up to. He was perhaps a celebrity in his circle of friends and among his alumni, if not in the wider community. It was amazing that she still remembered the name of his school after all these years. The website gave her immediate access to newsletters including photos taken at school events. To showcase students' track records and achievements, most schools were more than happy to make their information public. Margaret's guilty feeling of spying on Nathan was cut short as soon as she spotted a special issue about him.

He was indeed treated as a celebrity at his alma mater. In the photo album of the swimming gala in 2011, Nathan posed as a guest speaker and a medal presenter—in other words, a key person at the event. Margaret noticed that he had gained a few pounds and had grown a faint moustache, but otherwise he looked quite the same as he did twenty-four years ago. One photo showed him standing beside a banner with big Chinese characters welcoming him back to his old school. He carried his usual big grin in all these photos. Margaret could imagine him having a very busy day, talking to people whom he was meeting for the first time.

Just when Margaret was about to take a break, her eyes were caught by a hyperlink to a video clip entitled "An interview with Mr. Nathan Chan." How could she resist the temptation of watching him in action again? In eight minutes, he talked to two young students who asked about his secrets to success. His answers were clear, to the point, and sincere. Margaret felt that he was eager to share his experience. The final question asked was what he missed the most. Whether it was due to Margaret's imagination or a slight delay in the streaming of the video clip, Nathan gave a moment of hesitation. Why did he not give his answer promptly as he did with all other questions? Was he going to say something personal? Would he say what he missed most was the summer he spent with his girlfriend? The answer he finally gave was disappointingly boring: what he missed most was his school and his teachers.

Unlike the photos that were static, the video gave a new perspective. Margaret heard the same voice, but this older Nathan seemed so much more organised and eloquent. People would of course mature, but somehow Margaret felt that she was watching a rather different person whose mannerisms were entirely distant from what she remembered. Why was he so conscious of what he said and how he looked? Why wasn't he as carefree as before?

The newsletter also mentioned his profession, which had nothing to do with sports. Nathan introduced himself as a merchandiser working for a fashion company called Flaming. *Flaming? What an odd name.* It was probably a very small local company.

When she was done with her ex-boyfriend, Margaret turned to the paper that had fallen from the photos the night before. Staring at her own handwriting, her mind took her back to that night. Over the phone, Dominic dictated his address, urging Margaret for help. Even though she did not end up going to his home, it was amazing that she was still in possession of this paper. But where would this address take her? Without indicating which flat, would she be able to find Dominic? Margaret remembered asking for more information but was told that it would do. She looked at the name of the street again—Queen's Road West—an area that she did not know very well. Thanks to the advent of technology, almost immediately, she could see where it was and what the neighbourhood looked like. The ease of seeing her friend's street on her computer created an illusion of a speedy reunion.

Very quickly, a few scenarios popped up in her mind. Wouldn't it be perfect if Dominic came to answer the door himself? She would then walk into his flat, and together they would start reminiscing about the old days. What a preposterous idea! Margaret involuntarily shook her head and felt uneasy with her childish fantasy. For one thing, Margaret wouldn't be surprised if Dominic no longer lived there. Even if he did, would he recognise her? Suddenly, his voice of urgency rang loud in her head, calling for her help. Whether or not Dominic still lived there, Margaret decided that she had to make this overdue visit.

With a destination in mind, Margaret felt more relaxed and could think better. It then dawned on her why the name Flaming sounded funny. Nathan wouldn't have been working for a company with such a silly name. Those young fellows who interviewed him had to have made a mistake and didn't even bother to spell-check. He had to be working for Flamingo, which was a very famous fashion company in Hong Kong. Established in the 1970s, the company had been selling high fashion in hotel arcades and high-end shopping malls, all of them in the commercial and financial districts. How could she have missed the error? A small and harmless typing mistake had indeed made a huge difference in the meanings and implications of the two words.

Margaret quickly went back to her computer and did a new search. The company website was found, but unfortunately, neither staff names nor photos were shown. Beaten by this unsuccessful attempt, Margaret wondered what she could do next. What she saw in the interview was an elegantly dressed middle-aged man who seemed a rather well-to-do businessman. Nothing fancy, a well-cut black suit with a pink tie. Knowing that the company was trying to expand its market in China, he would perhaps be required to make frequent trips there. Like her, Nathan was perhaps also a well-travelled global citizen actively participating in social media in the name of his company. And she was right this time! By typing his name and the name of his company, Margaret found his social webpage.

A gentle message would entice him to respond. She wrote:

> *Dear Nathan,*
>
> *It's been such a long time since we last saw each other; the last time was when you saw me off at the Kai Tak Airport. I can't believe it's already that long; even the airport exists no more.*
>
> *If you want to keep in touch like I do, please send me a message. But if you decide to stay away, I perfectly understand why.*
>
> *Here's my photo and the one you gave me to help you remember who I am, if they make any sense to you. I hope you will write to me.*
>
> *Yours truly,*
>
> *Margaret*

There was no reason why Margaret signed the message "Yours truly," but that's what she did. If he chose to ignore her message or block her from his page, would Margaret truly understand why, or would she feel hurt?

To improve the chances of winning his trust, and to stop him from deleting her message, she thought it a good idea to attach his photo. People wouldn't usually delete their own face, would they? Margaret captured an image of the photo on her phone. Though it came out with a rather low resolution, she wasn't bothered. Not even the original was perfect; the old photo was a little blurred and yellowish, somehow a reflection of Margaret's fading memory.

Margaret quickly dressed and made her way to Queen's Road West on the MTR. At the last station on the Island Line, she asked for directions at the ticket office.

"It's a very long road. Which number are you looking for?"

"One three four."

"It will take at least fifteen minutes to walk there. You can take a taxi if you are in a hurry."

Margaret was in no hurry. How could she be if she had waited all these years? Besides, competing for a taxi with other passengers wasn't what Margaret was good at. She chose to walk. It was the right decision, since walking there would give her time to reflect on her unusual behaviour. Margaret wasn't sure what she was looking for in this trip. Was it only a reunion with an old friend, or was it something else? She had not even planned what to say to Dominic if she did see him again.

All Margaret wanted was to remember this day, and one way of making sure that she did was to take photos. Along the way were shops that were rather typical of the district, although they were not commonly found in this cosmopolitan city. There were a few shops selling dried seafood, and a few others specialising in Chinese herbal medicine. Because of its nostalgic feeling, it was quite normal for Margaret to take photos of the street from time to time. She was not the only one taking pictures. Along the way were tourists strolling on their own or in pairs, consulting a guidebook or taking snapshots of their surroundings. With her foreign look, Margaret easily blended in as one of them.

As she was getting close to the address, she couldn't help imagining the different scenarios again. The street looked exactly the same as what she had seen on her computer. This part of the street looked very interesting, with a few shops selling colourful goods. Margaret's knowledge of local products was limited, but she guessed they had to be some kind of offerings for gods and ancestors who were worshipped because of their supernatural power. Being displayed in the shops were candles, joss sticks, and paper offerings in yellow and red.

Margaret found the number easily. It was a low-rise of five storeys, a typical *Tong lau* built between the 1950s and the 1960s, with a wrought-iron entrance. On the exterior wall was a panel of doorbells for the different units. She pressed the one marked "third floor" and waited. No answer. She pressed again, and still there was no answer. Normally she would not speak to strangers, but since she had come a long way, she had no choice but to seek help from the shopkeeper who started looking her way.

"Do you know the people living on the third floor?" asked Margaret in her flawless Cantonese.

"No, I don't."

"Do you know if there's a caretaker in the building?"

"No, I don't think so."

Had a passerby not come over and pressed all the doorbells, she would have given up. Not knowing why he did that, she simply stared at him.

"Just try," said the man with a shrug. "Someone might open the door for you."

And he was right; someone answered the door. Through the intercom, Margaret told the person she was calling at the unit on the third floor. The door was immediately opened. No questions and no identity check! Margaret couldn't believe her luck. She didn't expect she would get help from a stranger after her first encounter with the unfriendly shopkeeper who seemed indifferent to her predicament.

She walked up the stairway, which was not very wide but looked clean enough. There was no littering and no funny smell. Seeing that there was only one door on each floor, Margaret understood why the address did not indicate the number of the flat. The door on the third floor was made of rusty iron and had bars that allowed passersby to see through. There was no second door to block the interior. The fact that Margaret could peer into the flat made her think that somebody had to be home. The doorbell that Margaret pressed gave a loud and piercing sound. A long wait confirmed that nobody was home. It was peculiar to let others look into your flat as if it were on display. Margaret couldn't understand why people chose to live in a flat without a proper door, but human behaviour, including hers, was sometimes hard to explain.

Margaret couldn't think of any other options than making inquiries. She walked one floor up to see if she could talk to anyone. After trying all the upper floors without meeting a single soul, she walked down with a heavy heart. When Margaret was positioned three or four steps above the third floor, she had a good view of the interior of the flat. On the left of the small entrance was an old writing desk stacked with papers and boxes of all sizes. Against the wall was a wooden shelf loaded with a number of old books and many other items that appeared ancient. Nothing much could be seen on the right, but there seemed to be an open space somewhere out there, perhaps a small balcony. Margaret saw enough to be able to conclude that either the flat was very small and full of clutter, or it had a very weird layout. There seemed to be many walls and narrow corridors inside. Having studied the flat for a good while, Margaret began walking down the stairs, and this time she took a much slower pace.

Having learnt her lesson from the man who offered help, Margaret pressed every doorbell as she was descending from floor to floor. *Just try. And why not?* But Margaret received no answer; this time, not even the person who opened the main gate for her responded. She had perhaps no other choice but to leave a note, the one that she had prepared. It was a handwritten note, written in very similar wording as the message she had composed for Nathan. As she was pushing open the front door and saw the mailboxes of each floor in front of her, Margaret changed her mind. She could not make herself put the note into the mailbox, though not because it would involve the risk of writing to the wrong person. Rather, it was the living environment she saw that had changed her thinking. If Dominic was still living in this building, he wouldn't be pleased with her visit. He wouldn't feel proud of his place now. Taking residence in this building now as opposed to what he had done twenty years ago would be a completely different matter. It would mean the same life, one that had become stagnant in a humble environment. It would mean a difficult life with no change and no hope. He wouldn't be pleased about it.

Putting the note back into her bag, Margaret walked into the street where she met the same shopkeeper again. His hostility didn't stop her from making a last attempt at probing for information though.

"Do you have any idea how old the people are, you know, those who live on the third floor?"

"No."

Margaret sensed a cold and unfriendly tone but thanked him regardless. Queen's Road West is a one-way street with two lanes. Very easily, she crossed the road where she could take a few snapshots of the building's exterior. The shopkeeper looked at her with ever more suspicion. But why would Margaret care for someone she would never see again?

On her way back to the MTR station, Margaret reflected on all the scenarios she had come up with before making this expedition, but none of them came close to what she experienced. She didn't expect to be able to see the inside of the flat without entering it. This made her feel ever more like an outsider, an unwelcome intruder, one who had never entered Dominic's life, not when she was given the chance of doing so twenty years ago, and certainly not now. When she considered the opportunity that was once so generously given and yet not taken up, her mind was suddenly filled with nothing but remorse.

She had yet another fifteen minutes to make sense of her experience. As she walked towards the train station, she kept searching for a face among the passersby who happened to cross her path. Could one of them belong to the person whom she came all the way to see? Her common sense told her that the chances of bumping into Dominic in the street were almost nonexistent; it was like finding a needle in a haystack. If she had never bumped into him in the last twenty years, what made her think that it would happen now? But all the same, she kept looking at every possible face while trying to imagine what her friend would now look like. She looked hard at any passerby of his age. The more she concentrated, the more blurred her eyes became.

When the station came into sight, she understood that it was time to admit her failure. Other than taking a few pictures, she had achieved nothing. Suddenly, she remembered that she did not even take out his photo from the storeroom. It still remained in that dark corner. Tears welled up in her eyes, and she had to fight hard to control herself. Margaret supposed that she could have got to know Dominic better if she had wanted to, but the fact was she was so indulged with her own existence that she tended to overlook other people's needs. She was rather insensitive in those years, but it was also her insensitivity that gave her the freedom to choose what she liked. She missed the years when it was absolutely all right to care for nobody's feelings but her own.

PART II
SUMMER 1989
HONG KONG

FRIENDS

It was a special summer. It was a summer with no school and no obligations; it was a summer to spend with friends. It was Margaret's last summer as a teenager in Hong Kong before her family moved to Canada. Very soon, she would begin a new chapter of life, leaving the old one behind. But Margaret knew that there wouldn't be much to look back on unless something happened now.

Her yearning for new experiences kept her busy. She constantly looked for new activities so she could spend time with her friends away from her mother's watchful eyes. Also, she couldn't wait to grow up so that she could understand why her mother was glued to the TV, watching the news nervously all day long.

"Oh my god, the tanks will be in Hong Kong any minute now," screamed her mother in her Canadian accent. How Margaret hated the fact that her family spoke English in different accents—Mom in her Canadian accent, Dad in his educated Hong Kong accent, and she in her expatriate international accent, which meant an accent with no roots.

"No, they won't." Margaret had to calm her mother down, not only because she knew her mother would get worse if she did not, but she also knew that it wouldn't happen as long as Hong Kong remained a British colony.

"What makes you so sure?"

"I just do." Margaret's answers to most of her mother's questions were short and blunt. It wasn't because Margaret didn't love her mother; she was obliged to be a difficult daughter. Didn't all her friends behave in the same way? Margaret wouldn't mind her mother's nagging, lecturing, spying, eavesdropping, and the like. There was no question of her motive: Betty had to protect her only daughter. What she saw on the TV in the past few days drew out her mother's instincts and put her on high alert.

"I am feeling certain about my decision. We must get out of Hong Kong before the situation gets nasty," said Betty.

"Like what?"

"If the government doesn't like people marching on the streets and decides to impose a curfew, our freedoms will be restricted."

"It won't happen." Margaret stuck with her standard three-word answer.

"Why not? What's happening in China now will happen in Hong Kong one day."

"But we are not in China." Margaret made an exception to the length of her answer in order to stop her mother from talking nonsense.

"True. We'll get out of here before that happens. We are lucky that we can move back to Canada. I feel so sorry for our friends and our neighbours. They are such nice people. What will happen to them? Where can Mr. and Mrs. Chan go? What future is there for their kids?"

"I'm going." Margaret announced her departure without waiting for her mother to drag on the topic.

"Where are you going?"

"Japanese class."

"Are you still taking Japanese lessons? Why are you still going? Didn't I tell you to quit?"

"Why?"

"You won't need Japanese in Canada. If you want to learn a foreign language, French will come in more useful."

"Not interested."

"It must be Cindy who talked you into it. I know she is a bad influence." Being one of Margaret's good friends at school, she took the blame for almost any misbehaviour of her only daughter.

"Bye, Mom."

Margaret simply dashed off, knowing that another look at her mother would risk a further delay.

"Will you be home for dinner?"

Margaret was already in the lift lobby and couldn't be bothered to go back to remind her that they were eating out. She had already told her mother that it was Cindy's birthday. It would be a lot of fun. Not only was Cindy good at telling jokes, but they had also invited their new friend from the Japanese class. What was her name again? Why didn't she go by an English name like all of her classmates and family friends? Margaret found it exceptionally difficult to remember names in Chinese even though she was fluent in Cantonese.

Another thing Margaret couldn't understand was why her mother was so against Cindy. Was it because Cindy did not perform particularly well at school? Or was it because once she had a fit of laughter, it was uncontrollable until her belly ached so much that she started crying? No, neither reason was sufficient to explain why her mother was so cold to Cindy every time she came to their home. Anyway, Cindy had made it very clear that she would not visit her home again. Visiting Margaret in Canada would also be out of the question. What a shame! Margaret knew that it would be fun to take Cindy places.

There was no time for any sentimental ideas. At the entrance of the YWCA, Cindy was studying her notes. Margaret and her friends always entered and left the class together to show solidarity. Being the youngest in class, they felt a little intimated by other students who appeared mature and serious about their studies.

"Hi, Cindy! Sorry to keep you waiting," greeted Margaret.

Cindy looked at her watch and said, "That's okay. I came early to study for the Kana test."

"Oh no! I completely forgot about the test. Mom has been nagging me the whole day. I hardly had time to pick up my notes. What shall I do?"

"Take it easy. Just sit close to me and copy whatever you can, although I do not know any better than you do."

"Oh, it won't be right. What if we are caught?"

"Who cares? Learning Japanese is only for fun. We just want to be able to read our Japanese comics. I don't see why the teacher is so serious about it." It was probably Cindy's couldn't-care-the-less attitude that Margaret's mother did not approve of.

"Some of our classmates are very keen and they take the course very seriously. They might want to use the language for something other than reading comics," Margaret said of their scholarly classmates.

"I know. Such idiots. What are they studying so hard in the summer for? They know nothing about the little pleasures that make life so much more colourful."

"I don't suppose they learn Japanese for fun. They must be learning it for their future."

"That really beats me. How can we plan ten, twenty years down the line when we don't even know what to study in the university?"

"Maybe they do. Anyway, where's Tsz Ping?"

"You mean Tsz Ching? She'll be here any minute. She called me just before I left home, saying that she's running late."

"I am glad you remember her name. I have no memory space for Chinese names."

"You can't be that bad, can you? I mean, you never have a problem speaking Chinese."

"Speaking it is different. It's the names I have a problem with. Maybe because I don't study Chinese history, calling people by their Chinese names is hard work for me."

They had no time to further discuss the issue of names. Tsz Ching arrived in her new jeans and new sneakers. They hadn't seen this style before.

"I'm sorry. I was trying to wrap it up nicely. Happy birthday." Tsz Ching was out of breath and had a problem speaking coherently.

"Thank you. I love the wrapping paper. It has my favourite Hello Kitty print. Can I open it?"

"Sure. I hope you like it. It's a small and inexpensive gift. You might like the wrapping paper more than the gift."

"Don't worry. I am not fussy."

To avoid any further delay, Margaret suggested, "We'd better go to our class first. Cindy can open her presents later. I have one for you too."

"Oh, I'm not sure if I can focus on the test anymore." Cindy could not conceal her excitement. "Tsz Ching, I nearly forgot to say that I like your new outfit. Where do you buy your clothes?"

"In Mongkok. They are very cheap. I can take you to my favourite shops."

"Let's go there one day. Margaret, are you interested?"

Their talk suddenly came to a stop on entering a classroom that was filled with silence.

MISUNDERSTANDINGS

The Kana test turned out to be extremely easy; it wasn't much of a test. Students were allowed to discuss with each other; they could even consult the textbook, not only once, but as many as three times if they wanted to during the test. But how could the teacher monitor everyone? So, the test was conducted in such a relaxed manner that it was a misnomer to call it as such.

Cindy, who announced to the teacher on arrival that it was her birthday, claimed the credit as soon as they were seated in a pizza restaurant. "You must thank me for bringing you luck. He would not give such an easy test if it had not been my birthday."

"Your birthday has nothing to do with how the test was conducted," Margaret protested.

"Of course it does."

"No, it doesn't."

Tsz Ching did not want the fight to go on. "Stop arguing, the two of you. The test is done, and we will surely pass it. So, what's there to argue about? Shouldn't we celebrate? One, that we passed the test, and two, that today is our friend Cindy's birthday. Let's order food. I am starving."

"Okay," Margaret agreed reluctantly.

Although there was no point to insist on her thinking, Margaret knew the real reason behind the teacher's leniency. It was her own charm rather than Cindy's birthday that melted the heart of the teacher. During her two friends' toilet break, Margaret confessed that she was so preoccupied with moving to another country that she had completely forgotten about the test. She explained with tears in her eyes that there were too many errands to run, giving a candid and sincere apology. How could a young male teacher have the heart to scold someone like Margaret? Besides, she appeared innocent and irresistibly beautiful. Margaret had a tall and slender figure. At five foot eight, she was much taller than her peers. Her long brown hair was always well-combed. Whether she wore a ponytail or let her hair down, she looked gorgeous. She had the skin of her mother—fair and not easily tanned. Her features combined those of her parents. Her eyes were of the right size, not intimidatingly large. Anyone who saw her for the first time would naturally want to protect someone who looked so sweet and harmless.

Margaret wasn't interested in talking more about the test and pretended to study the menu. Tsz Ching knew exactly what to order—a big pizza with pepperoni, cheese, and mushrooms, a spaghetti Bolognese, and one serving at the salad bar.

"Shall we make it two? I like salad," suggested Margaret.

"No, we can save some money." Tsz Ching then leaned over and whispered, "One of my classmates is working here part-time. I'm pretty sure he's on duty today. When I see him, I can ask him to slip another bowl on our table when the manager is not paying attention."

"Isn't it cheating? I like it though. A free salad." Cindy started clapping her hands excitedly.

"Shush." Tsz Ching was quick at keeping Cindy under control before other customers started to look at them.

"Relax. No one heard us," said Cindy.

"If your friend works here, he can perhaps give us a free salad, like something on the house," said Margaret.

Tsz Ching straightened her back, then her face, before giving her reply in a serious tone, "I wouldn't go that far. This classmate of mine belongs to the category of 'good students,' if you see what I mean. He works very hard, never skips school, and always does his best. I am not even sure if he will go along with our plan."

"Let's try. I can't wait to convert a saint into an evil-doer," said Cindy excitedly.

"Why can't we simply order it ourselves?" Margaret said rather unhappily, feeling that she was being sidelined in this salad-bar scenario. "I don't want to get your classmate into trouble." For some reason, she felt sorry for dragging Tsz Ching's classmate into their naughty act.

"But it's so exciting, isn't it? I'm sure we can get away with it," assured Tsz Ching. "There he is. He's coming over. Just keep talking and pretend that it's a chance meeting."

The warning came hopelessly late. Cindy's giggles were ringing in the air and wouldn't have stopped had Margaret not kicked her under the table.

When Tsz Ching's classmate arrived at their table, Cindy was rubbing her shin, complaining how brutal the kick was. Margaret retreated into the corner of the booth and sulked, making it very clear that she played no part in their evil plot. What she didn't realise was that her aloof and detached manner elevated her attractiveness.

"Hi, Dominic, I almost forgot you work here. Come and meet my friends. This is Cindy. Over there is Margaret." Cindy started giggling in the middle of Tsz Ching's introduction.

"What's the matter with you?" asked Tsz Ching.

Cindy breathed out these words as she was trying to suppress another outburst. "But . . . but it's a girl's name."

"Mine is spelled D O M I N I C."

"Don't mind her, Dominic. Cindy is rather silly," said Tsz Ching.

"That's okay." For one reason or another, he suddenly turned to Margaret and asked, "How can I help you?"

All along, they had been speaking in Cantonese, so his broken, robotic English triggered Cindy to start laughing again. She struggled very hard to say this before a second fit of laughter: "Why did you speak English to her? Margaret speaks perfect Cantonese."

Margaret felt sorry witnessing what happened to this new friend named Dominic. She knew Cindy well enough to know that her laugh would linger for some time. There was nothing they could do to make her stop. Besides, Cindy's laughter was contagious; very soon, they all laughed with her.

But this shared mirth did wonders. Not only did Dominic stop feeling embarrassed, he even agreed to comply with their request. How Tsz Ching managed to convince him, neither Margaret nor Cindy was aware of. All she did was take him aside for a short talk. By the time Margaret and Tsz Ching walked towards the salad bar, Cindy was quite composed, lounging on her padded seat, busily wiping away tears of laughter.

Margaret and Tsz Ching filled their bowls the best they could. Most customers treated the self-service activity like a game or a competition. To make the most of the sole visit, everyone piled up as much as their skills would allow them to. The two girls put some vegetables at the bottom. They then poured a generous amount of salad dressing on top before stacking another layer of choices. Similar to most people, Margaret and Tsz Ching finished their presentation by sprinkling breadcrumbs and bacon flakes around the edge of the bowl. Margaret had a lot of fun decorating the food. Eating was secondary.

Walking back was a balancing act that required high concentration. Before they knew it, Dominic snatched the bowls out of their hands and laid them on his tray. Without saying a word, he placed them on their table.

He said in English, "Enjoy your meal."

"Amazing!" exclaimed Tsz Ching.

"What's amazing about it? I can pile up twice as much." Cindy couldn't help boasting about her salad-bar skills.

"I wasn't talking about the salad. I meant Dominic. Do you know how different he behaves today? For him to get so involved, he must be attracted to one of us."

They both started looking at Margaret's way. Then they looked at each other and nodded in a meaningful way.

"What are the two of you trying to say? I didn't even look at your friend."

"He's also your friend now," Tsz Ching reminded Margaret.

"Definitely your friend." Cindy was also nodding her head, as if she wanted to give more weight to the phrase.

"Can you cut it out now? It's all nonsense. I shouldn't be the centre of attention. It's Cindy's birthday. We should be talking about her, not me," Margaret said, hoping to divert her friends' attention.

"Don't worry. I have everything organised. It's convenient to have a friend working here." Tsz Ching gave a cheeky smile. Before they had the chance to ask what she meant, she snapped her fingers in Dominic's direction. This had to be their secret signal; Dominic disappeared into the kitchen.

They had no time to guess what was to come. A birthday cake landed on their table. Tsz Ching was really an excellent organiser, paying attention to every single detail. Cindy was about to hug Tsz Ching when she saw the cake was mistakenly put in front of Margaret. Everyone froze.

Without waiting for anyone to react, Margaret said, "It's Cindy's birthday. If you want to celebrate my birthday, you'll have to come to Canada."

Margaret did her best to save the embarrassing situation, for she felt partly responsible for Dominic's clumsy behaviour. It wasn't the first time that misunderstandings like this had happened. Margaret seemed to have a lot of power over people, particularly the opposite sex, as if they were under her spell. Boys always wanted to win her trust, and perhaps her heart too.

She leaned over to Cindy and pecked her on the cheek. "Happy birthday! This is for you." Margaret passed a little box tied with a red ribbon to her friend.

"Oh, thank you." Cindy opened the box in no time and found a pair of earrings inside.

Tsz Ching was more excited than any of them. "Oh, my God! Where did you buy them? They look so cool. Cindy, put them on. Quick."

"I'm sorry that I made a mistake. I thought it was your birthday," Dominic said, giving a delayed apology. "Did you say you will have your birthday in Canada? Why?"

"She's moving to Canada with her family when the summer is over. She will start her senior high school there." Cindy gave her answer while putting on the earrings. "Does anyone have a mirror?"

"Here you are." Tsz Ching was quick at supplying her with one. "Wow! You look gorgeous. You know what? If you wear those and a pair of high heels, and of course the right dress, I am sure you can get by the security guards at any disco. Nobody's going to check your ID."

"Disco?" Margaret and Cindy repeated the word in unison.

"Didn't I tell you that one of my classmates is now working at a disco? We can go there for free if you want to."

"Oh, let's do that before Margaret leaves Hong Kong. I don't know how to dance, but it will be fun to go together," urged Cindy.

Margaret looked at Tsz Ching and said with envy, "You surely have a lot of friends, and they are all very nice to you." Stealing a glance at Dominic, Margaret could tell what she had said made him blush.

This time, Dominic managed not to show his embarrassment and asked, "Can I go with you?"

On hearing this, the three girls burst into laughter again. Poor Dominic, he had no idea what was so funny about his simple request.

A NEW EXPERIENCE

In the following week, Margaret was busy shopping for clothes and makeup. She wanted to look her best at her first disco dance. This was, of course, done without her mother's knowledge. Betty was given a different story: her daughter needed to buy some souvenirs from Hong Kong to give to her new friends in Canada.

Each and every shopping trip was an eye-opener for Margaret. Being used to shopping for clothes in Japanese department stores under her mother's close supervision, Margaret was amazed to pay one-quarter of the price for similar styles in the Mongkok area. She could find all the young and trendy apparel in those little shops that fit not more than five people at a time. At her age, when quality materials or workmanship was of little concern, Margaret was happy that she could afford buying a lot of what she liked.

Margaret had no problem choosing what to wear. She knew exactly what suited her. Her problem was of a different kind. How was she going to leave home in her disco outfit without causing any suspicion? Luckily, Tsz Ching was so streetwise that it took her no time to come up with a solution.

"Easy, just bring everything to my place. We will get changed and do our makeup together. My mother won't be home."

So, it was arranged that all three girls made preparations together at Tsz Ching's place. They would spend the morning trying out all the clothes they bought over the week and experimenting them with the palettes of eye colours and lipsticks. Having watched how her mother applied makeup over the years, Margaret did her best to turn everyone into great beauties.

They had a lot of fun messing around with anything they got hold of—clothes, shoes, accessories, hair gel, and makeup.

When they were finally ready to leave, they all looked quite mature. Wearing a one-piece dress, high heels, and sparkling jewellery, they no longer had the look of innocent school kids; instead, they now looked so gorgeous and attractive that people would surely turn their heads to admire their youth and beauty.

The first person they charmed was the caretaker. As soon as they stepped out of the lift, he whistled, "Hi, gorgeous. Where are you off to?"

"Disco." Tsz Ching seemed to know him quite well. "We are going to the disco."

"Shouldn't you be studying at home?" The caretaker could not take his eyes off them and perhaps wanted to keep them for as long as he could. "I'll tell your mother when she gets home."

"Do as you please. She knows where I'm going. Besides, I'll be home long before she does." Tsz Ching was already walking away with her friends, holding their hands in hers. As they were leaving the building, she turned back and stuck her tongue out at the caretaker. In an instant of making a face, she suddenly looked a naughty child again.

"You haven't told your mother, have you?" asked Margaret.

"No, but she wouldn't mind even if she knew."

"You mean your mother will not get angry if she finds out that you've been to a disco and that you haven't asked her for her approval?"

"No, why would she be upset? I never get angry when she stays out late. I only got mad at her once when I was ten. She came home at three in the morning and was so drunk that I thought she was going to die. I kept crying as I was helping to clean up the mess she made. Afterwards, we had a nice, long talk. Then we promised to be nice and reasonable to each other."

"Meaning?" Cindy couldn't help probing to encourage more information. Tsz Ching did not talk much about her parents. In fact, she had never mentioned her father in the past few months of their acquaintance. It was the first time they heard her talk about her mother.

"We agreed that as long as we do not stay out overnight, it'll be fine," Tsz Ching said with a shrug as she was holding the door of a taxi for her friends to get in. To the driver, she said, "Stanley Street, please."

They were already sitting in a taxi heading their way to the disco when Margaret asked one more question about Tsz Ching and her mother's agreement. "Did you say *we*?"

"It's only fair that the rule applies to both of us. Don't you think?" Tsz Ching looked both of her friends in their eyes. Without getting a response, she continued talking in a slightly raised voice, "Oh my gosh, we are so late. Dominic must be getting impatient now."

"Don't worry," assured Cindy. "As long as Margaret is here with us, he'll never get mad."

"It's so true. You know what? He can't stop talking about Margaret whenever we have the chance to talk at school." At this point, Tsz Ching couldn't help rolling her eyes. "He can't take his mind off this disco date. I bet he will just hang around Margaret."

"What do I have to do with him?" protested Margaret.

"I won't let him," Cindy also protested at the same time but for a different reason. "The idea is for us girls to have fun together."

"Agreed," echoed everyone.

The agreement held valid for only thirty minutes before they bumped into another friend of Tsz Ching's. In half an hour, they managed to enter the disco, order drinks, and find a table as their base without a fuss. Not even Dominic's causal outfit aroused any suspicion. They were let in without an ID check.

Margaret had been looking forward to spending an exciting summer before starting high school in Canada. All she wanted was some fun and perhaps a new experience. What she wasn't aware of was that something extraordinary was happening. It would be years later before she came to understand that it wasn't her personal experience, but an historical event that struck unpleasantly close to home.

Tsz Ching did not arrange to meet anyone else at the disco, although she knew one of her friends went there fairly regularly in the summer. He wasn't exactly a friend; Nathan was her swimming coach. For a long time, Tsz Ching's wish was to take up a sport activity that she could play well enough to be able to compete and win. Her wish at last came true when she met Nathan in an interschool swimming competition and that he agreed to coach her once a week.

On the day she came to cheer for her school team, Tsz Ching's attention was captured by Nathan's streamlined body propelling forward as if he were sliding in the water. As a cheerleader, she had watched many swimming competitions, but she had never seen a top swimmer like Nathan. Watching him swim at a fast speed gave her such an exciting feeling that Tsz Ching stopped cheering for her team. She even slipped away and found an opportunity to speak with him over the break. Nathan ignored her at first, thinking that she was yet another fan of his, but then he started to pay her some attention when he realised that she had approached him for a different reason. Nathan had been training all along to compete, but he had never trained anyone, so Tsz Ching's request for swimming lessons interested him.

"Tell me why you want to take swimming lessons with me," asked Nathan. "Don't you have a coach for your school team?"

"But I'm not on my school team—not yet," said Tsz Ching.

"That's interesting," said Nathan as he started looking at Tsz Ching for the first time. What he saw in front of him was a skinny girl with braces in her mouth. "So, what are you here for?"

"I came as a cheerleader," said Tsz Ching. "Next time when I come, I want somebody to cheer for me."

"Good for you. But can you swim?" asked Nathan.

"Sure."

"In what style?"

"Front crawl and breaststroke," said Tsz Ching.

"Good. What's your record?"

"I dunno," said Tsz Ching. "I never pay attention to it." Seeing that Nathan started knitting his eyebrows, she added, "But I can swim faster than anyone on the cheering team."

"Really!" said Nathan. "How about this: why don't you come to the training centre and let me check how fast you can swim? We'll then decide what to do. Is that okay?"

"Sure. When shall I come?" asked Tsz Ching.

"How about next Wednesday at four o'clock? I practise every day from five to seven."

"You practise every day?"

"Of course, you'll have to do the same if you want to compete and have your school friends cheer for you."

That was the first conversation Tsz Ching had with Nathan. How long ago was that? Would that be two years earlier? She was trying to recall the details soon after she caught sight of him on the dance floor. When Nathan finally looked in her direction, Tsz Ching waved to say hello. Almost immediately, he ran over to their table, bringing with him another young bloke.

There were six of them now, and it took a while to introduce themselves. Each introduction lasted for a few attempts of high-pitched yelling with loud music in the background. When it was Margaret's turn, an exchange of names between her and Nathan was exceptionally long. If she had not giggled upon Nathan saying something in her ear, her friends would have thought that she had simply missed hearing his name. They saw an immediate development of friendship. That much was clear, but nobody understood why and what was going on.

Ignoring the friend he brought with him, Nathan took Margaret's hand and led her onto the dance floor. "Come, this is my favourite song."

"Did you see that?" exclaimed Cindy. "They are holding hands."

"That is what your partner does when he invites you for a dance," said Tsz Ching.

"Really?" Cindy said in a doubtful voice. "But they only met today. I think something's going on."

"I think so too," said Dominic.

"What are you talking about?" asked Alan, who was completely at the mercy of his new friends' kindness now that he was abandoned. "I can't hear you."

"Nothing," said Cindy.

"Do you want to dance?" asked Alan.

"You mean like them?" said Cindy with her fingers tightly interlocking with each other. "No, thank you."

"How about a drink for everyone?" asked Alan.

"That would be nice," said Tsz Ching.

"Not for me," said Dominic.

"Come on, I'll do this round, and you'll do the next one," said Alan. "It'll be a while before they join us. Let's enjoy ourselves."

"What makes you think so?" asked Dominic.

"What makes me think what?" asked Alan.

"They will keep dancing?" asked Cindy.

"Sure," said Alan. "Do you think Nathan is attracted to every girl he meets for the first time? I've never seen him get so attached on a first date."

"It's nobody's date," shouted Cindy. "We made a deal of staying close to each other. Now look at what your friend has done to us. He's spoilt our fun."

"And mine too. Anyway, we can still enjoy ourselves without them. What do you think?" Alan gently elbowed Dominic as he was saying the last sentence.

"Don't touch me." Dominic jumped and quickly removed his elbow from the table.

"What's wrong with you? I was only trying to be nice," said Alan.

"Don't mind him," said Cindy. "Your friend has stolen his queen."

"Who's the queen? Oh, please tell me more." Alan pleaded for more gossip.

So, what happened in the next half an hour completely changed the group dynamics. Cindy and Alan first talked about their friends before turning their conversation to themselves. While they talked nonstop, Tsz Ching and Dominic were busy finishing their drinks and sulking. They neither talked nor made eye contact with each other. Occasionally, Tsz Ching directed her attention to the dance floor, searching for the two figures that intermittently appeared among the crowd.

It was as though the level of intimacy increased with the intensity of the music. By the third dance, Nathan was already holding Margaret by her waist, regardless of tempo or rhythm. At six foot two, Nathan had the right physique for Margaret to rest her head on his shoulder, and this was what she did in their first slow dance. It had been a long day for Margaret. Getting up at seven to prepare herself for this eventuality consumed a lot of energy, and she had not even eaten a proper meal. So, she naturally found it comforting to lay her head on Nathan's broad and muscular shoulders, which resulted from years of training in the water.

Leaning against a powerful body, Margaret was almost dozing off, when suddenly she felt a stream of warm air breathing into her ear. "You must be tired. Let me get you a drink."

Lifting up her head in order to make sense of these words, Margaret's eyes were met by a large and angular face. In a way, she was glad to have this face shielding off the disco lights that would have otherwise been too bright for her.

"No, I'm fine," said Margaret in her dreamy voice. "I want to dance a little longer."

"Do you call it dancing?" said Nathan. "Your legs hardly move."

"Oh, I'm sorry." Margaret quickly straightened her back, giving Nathan an embarrassed smile as she realised how she had been resting her body onto his for who knows how long. "It must be the high heels; they are hurting me."

"That's all right. I like the smell of your hair. But still, I think we should rest a little."

"Okay," said Margaret reluctantly, "if you insist."

"Yes, I do. Besides, I think we are done with being anti-social for the day."

"Oh, I forgot we girls are supposed to have fun together."

"I feel bad for leaving Alan on his own too."

"Let's go back and join them now."

"Wait," said Nathan. "Give me your phone number before we join them."

"But you can't call me at home," said Margaret.

"Why not?"

"Because my mother doesn't know anything about today."

"I won't tell her that you've been to a disco," said Nathan.

"That's not the point." Margaret began to sound a little agitated.

"What's the point then?" asked Nathan.

"The thing is, my mother won't expect me to get phone calls from a boy."

"Don't you have any male friends?"

"I do, but they are all friends from the church, and Mom knows all of them."

"Oh, I see. In that case, my sister can act as an operator," said Nathan. "I don't think her voice will arouse any suspicion. What do you say?"

"That's very naughty." Margaret paused for a while before she continued, "And clever of you."

Knowing that they had to join their friends did not in the least cause them to exchange their telephone numbers in great haste. They did so in a relaxed manner as they were dancing to a song with piano accompaniment, music that rarely played in a disco. The soft melody gave Margaret a great opportunity to lean onto Nathan's shoulders a little longer. By whispering and repeating two sets of numbers, they somehow managed to hypnotise each other into a state that they would most certainly comply with any request of their partner. It was at least true for Margaret. If Nathan had asked her not to leave Hong Kong at that moment, she would have given up on moving to Canada with her family.

Nathan's sentiments were, however, more complicated, and in a way hard to explain. His behaviour surprised both his friend and himself. At the age of eighteen, he was considered mature in both his actions and words. Years of training and occasional defeats in the pool had turned him into someone who was strong and adaptable. Not that he would allow himself to lose a game that he both enjoyed and felt proud of, but when he did, he showed great resilience. Each setback would only motivate him to train harder for the next competition.

Another reason for his maturity was his upbringing. Being born into a working-class family, he knew what life was like without sufficient resources. That was why the first meeting with Tsz Ching was so important to him, without which he wouldn't have had the chance to earn extra cash to acquire small luxuries, mostly for his own use, and sometimes for his little sister. Over the last two years, he had recruited as many as twenty students who paid high fees in return for his coaching. It had never occurred to Nathan that there was such a big demand for professional coaching in swimming until he met Tsz Ching. No wonder she was his lucky star. Didn't she bring Margaret to his life? Nathan fell in love with Margaret almost at first sight. No matter how much Nathan disliked this cliché, he had to accept it, and he was ready to be an object of ridicule.

It wasn't exactly Margaret's beauty that drew Nathan to her. Margaret was no doubt an attractive girl, but it had to be more than her physical appearance that did the trick. It wasn't easy to explain why Margaret was special, but she was truly different from other girls. Friends in his neighbourhood, or swimmers from fellow school teams, all had similar background to his. They were highly competitive, independent, and tough. Being so different from what he was used to, it was perhaps Margaret's softness that captured his body and soul completely.

It was also Margaret's middle-class, cross-cultural upbringing that made her mysteriously different. Nathan had no experience dealing with girls of her kind. One could almost tell another's background by asking a few personal details, such as address, name of school, and parent's occupation. Even without this information, people could still look out for other clues, such as the way a person dressed and talked. Margaret's last-minute decision to change back into her usual outfit of Japanese make gave her middle-class background away. The outfit she bought in Mongkok would have been all right for someone of an average height. At five foot eight, however, the dress looked way too short on Margaret; it made her look ridiculous. Both Cindy and Tsz Ching agreed that the dress did not look good on her, although only Tsz Ching knew why. Being more mature and sensitive of their family backgrounds, she understood that Margaret was too classy for a cheap imitation.

Still in their good mood, Margaret and Nathan were unprepared to join their friends in the middle of an argument. It wasn't clear who started it. By the time Margaret began sipping the drink Nathan bought her, everyone seemed to be in some sort of a debate.

"What's the point of going?" asked Cindy. "What do you expect to see?"

"I don't expect to see anything," said Dominic. "Do you think I just go for fun?"

"Then what are you looking for?" asked Alan.

"I'm not looking for anything," said Dominic in a raised voice. "What makes you think I go there for myself?"

"Then who are you doing this for?" It was Tsz Ching who posed the question this time. "It makes no sense to me, no sense at all."

"Of course, I'm going in support of the students." Dominic was definitely shouting by now. "And their parents too. Why do you all just think about yourselves?"

"What are you talking about?" asked Margaret, who was absolutely clueless about her friends' conversation. "And why do you all look so serious?"

Without the music in the background during a brief intermission, everyone heard her, but no one was in the right mood to tell Margaret the cause of their conflict.

After a long, awkward silence, it was Tsz Ching who finally spoke, "We've been talking about the students in Beijing. Dominic wants to go and join the march tomorrow."

"Is there a march tomorrow?" asked Margaret. "What is it for?"

"Did you not watch the television or read the paper?" asked Dominic in a challenging tone.

"Everyone has the right to do what they like," said Cindy. "Go ahead and join the march if you like, but don't spoil our party, and don't spoil our fun."

"I don't understand you people. How can you just think about yourselves?"

At this point, even his classmate couldn't help feeling embarrassed and wanted to stop this unfriendly exchange of views once and for all.

"Dominic, you have to be fair," said Tsz Ching. "You can't expect everyone to feel the same way you do. Cindy was right to say that we can all choose how we feel. Just don't force your idea on us. We are here to dance. I didn't invite you to come and talk about politics."

"What sort of dance is it? Did you dance?" asked Dominic with a chuckle of irony. "Nobody's been dancing except Margaret. Do you enjoy being here?" Dominic turned to look at everyone as he asked these questions.

Though harsh, there was some truth in what Dominic had said, and this induced a sense of guilt in Margaret. Before she had the chance to apologise, Cindy came to her defense.

"You can't blame Margaret for what she's here for. We arranged our disco trip especially for her."

"Why especially for Margaret?" asked Alan. "Is it your birthday, Margaret?"

"No, it's not her birthday," continued Cindy, "but what's going to happen is even more special."

Then, a glass fell and shattered on the floor, interrupting everyone's anticipation of Cindy's explanation. When they realised that it was too late to save the drink that had been carelessly knocked down by Margaret, Cindy screamed at the top of her voice, "How can you be so clumsy? Who's going to look after you in Canada?"

"Who's going to Canada?" asked Nathan. Anyone who listened closely would have heard a sense of urgency in his voice.

"No one," said Margaret without looking at anyone, particularly not at Nathan. "I mean, no one but me. Cindy was talking about me. I will move to Canada with my parents after the summer."

It was as though a bombshell had been dumped on him. Nathan's body started shaking beyond control. Without saying a word, he turned his head and ran out of the disco. It wasn't long before Margaret ran after him.

"What are we going to do now?" asked Alan. "Is this the end of our party? Are we supposed to go after them?"

"Don't be silly," said Tsz Ching. "Let them be on their own for a while."

"See what you've done, Dominic?" protested Cindy. "It's all because of you. They are going to be on their own without us, again."

The odd thing about life was that even though people did not quite know what was going to happen next, they all secretly wanted to be in control of their own destinies. There was always an illusion of directing the course of life through planning, plotting, and hoping. This was why Margaret's mother decided to leave Hong Kong for good, trusting that this was the best choice she had ever made for her daughter and the family. Margaret had never questioned her mother's decision, not even once, until now. How she wished she were staying!

"Why didn't you tell me earlier?" Margaret caught him saying as she was running a few paces behind.

"Stop running," said Margaret. "I can't run in my high heels."

Neither did Nathan stop running nor turn round to check on Margaret. He kept running, making several turns until he came to an alley. There were no shops or passersby in this alley except for empty bottles and cans waiting to be taken away.

It was difficult for Margaret to keep up with Nathan. She only managed to catch the last glimpse before losing sight of him. Having hesitated for a short while, she gathered courage to walk into the alley, for she knew this area quite well. Even though she had never walked down this way before, Margaret figured that this had to be one of those blind alleys. With no way out, Nathan had to be hidden somewhere behind the empty beer bottles. But what was he doing there?

As Margaret went further into the alley, she heard a sound but couldn't quite make out of its meaning. At first, she thought it was someone moaning or sighing, and this gave her a scare. However, her hesitation did not last for long. She decided to walk into it, just in case Nathan had been attacked and needed help. What she saw instead was beyond her understanding. Why was Nathan hitting his fist on the wall? Was he feeling unwell? Did he need help? Should Margaret call for an ambulance?

Before Margaret had time to work out the answers to any of these questions, Nathan said between his big sobs, "I don't want you to leave."

Margaret had several scenarios in her mind, but none came close to what she saw. She had nothing against people showing their emotions, but she would never have expected Nathan to be crying the way he did.

"Why didn't you tell me you're leaving soon?" said Nathan, still sobbing. The more he wanted to stop crying, the harder it was for him to control himself. He finally gave up holding his emotions and simply allowed his tears to wash away his frustration. He was angry to be told that his dream girl wouldn't be with him before long, and he was angry with himself for hopelessly falling in love. It was surely a pathetic sight that a strong young man had created.

After a while, Margaret moved up closer and touched Nathan on his shoulder. It was such a gentle touch that Nathan felt as though the current inside his body had suddenly changed. All his frustrations were gone; instead, his feelings became tender and soft. He turned round quickly and held Margaret very tightly in his arms. Knowing that she was forgiven, Margaret just let him hold her tight. He gradually brought her closer, diminishing the distance between them until her breasts pressed against his body. This physical closeness with a male body other than her father's brought a new sensation. She liked Nathan, but everything seemed to be moving too fast for her. This sudden intimacy also frightened her.

When Nathan finally stopped crying, turning his sobs into small gasps for air, Margaret gave him a gentle push and said, "I can't breathe."

"Sorry," said Nathan. Having released her, he immediately held Margaret's waist and turned her round as if they were dancing a tango. Now, Nathan was holding her tightly, resting his chin on Margaret's head. He took a deep breath, and said, "I'll remember your smell for the rest of my life."

Rather than flirting with him, which was something she had no experience with, Margaret teased, "Are you a dog or something?"

"You bet. Woof, woof." Nathan imitated a dog's barking sound as he brought one of Margaret's hands to his lips and started nibbling at it as if he were a wild animal. Very soon, the nibbling turned into kissing, first on her fingertips, then her hands and shoulders, and finally on her neck. If Margaret had turned her head to the right angle at that moment, Nathan would certainly have kissed her on her face and lips.

Rather than turning her head a little to give Nathan the chance, however, she turned round. Now seeing Nathan's face for the first time in natural light, she confirmed that she was not mistaken. He wasn't exactly handsome, but he certainly had his charm. He was big and strong. His eyes, mouth, ears, head, and limbs were big and to the right proportion. Nathan was more than a protector; he appeared as if he were someone Margaret could rely on for life.

"Am I your girlfriend?" asked Margaret.

"Yes, of course."

"Will I still be your girlfriend after I've left Hong Kong?"

"Let's change the topic, shall we?" said Nathan with a big frown. "Let's enjoy the moment and not think about anything else."

"But you know I won't be with you here for long," said Margaret in a worried tone. "You are of course more than welcome to come and spend time with me in Canada. What I mean is, we can't stay together every day, not like as if I lived in Hong Kong. I just hope that you don't think I intend to deceive you in any way—"

Margaret's monologue of confession was cut short by a slight pull from Nathan. Very skillfully, he turned Margaret and held her face with both hands, peering into her eyes, and started kissing her eyes, her nose, and her cheeks. When Nathan's lips finally moved towards Margaret's, there was a brief moment of struggle in her head. There was no time for any logical analysis; she let go of her defense and accepted an intimate connection with someone who had been a stranger a few hours before.

It was a short and sweet kiss, just the right kind for someone as inexperienced as Margaret. After the first kiss, they held each other for a little while before they kissed for a second time with greater intensity. No matter how much they wanted the time to hold there and then, the streetlamps lit up.

"It's getting dark," exclaimed Margaret. "It's already seven. We'd better go back before our friends start looking for us."

"Yeah, let's go back," sighed Nathan. "But you must promise me to come and watch me practise tomorrow."

"You mean swimming?" asked Margaret. "Sure. Can I bring Cindy with me?"

"Yes, of course. You can swim if you come early. Our practice starts at five o'clock, so if you come at three, we can swim together for a while."

"Do you have to give any swimming lessons tomorrow?"

"I can ask Alan to cover the class for me, just for once. Nothing's more important than spending time with you."

A RIVAL

None of them went to the march on the following day, except Dominic, so nobody knew what happened. Nobody cared; these young people were all too busy carrying on with their lives as usual. Besides, Beijing was too remote, nothing more than a patch on the map for them. For the two lovers, time was a great treasure, and Margaret and Nathan both knew that they didn't have much to waste. They just wanted to spend as much time together as their routine would allow them to. Nathan had never experienced such an overwhelming urge to capture the body and soul of a girl. He had no time to think about how to deal with Margaret's departure yet.

Margaret arrived at the sports complex with Cindy as arranged at three o'clock. At first, they couldn't locate the entrance and had to discuss which way to go. Cindy felt a gentle pat on her shoulder from the back.

"Hey, why are you here so early?" greeted Alan. "We won't start our practice until five."

"Nathan said we could come for a swim," said Cindy.

"He must have forgotten about his lessons."

"No, he did not," Cindy corrected him. "You are supposed to coach the students for him."

"Am I?" said Alan with annoyance. "It's not the first time he's done this to me. Every time when he comes across," Alan took a quick glance at Margaret before he carried on, "something interesting, he dumps his work on me."

Margaret thought she'd better not ask Alan what he meant by *something interesting*. She simply apologised. "I'm sorry."

"What did you say sorry for?" said Alan. "It's not your fault."

Hoping she could cheer him up, Cindy said with a big wink, "Let me be your assistant coach."

"Do you swim well?" asked Alan.

"You'll see," said Cindy as she was holding Margaret and Alan by the hand, leading the way into the hallway to the changing rooms.

"Do you think," asked Margaret as soon as they walked into the female changing rooms, "Alan is mad at us?"

"No, don't worry," assured Cindy.

"How can you tell?"

"Of course, I do know him rather well by now. How do you think I passed the time when you and Nathan enjoyed yourselves yesterday?" said Cindy with a big wink. "Both Tsz Ching and Dominic were so upset that they didn't talk much. In a way, I preferred them keeping silent. Every time Dominic spoke, he talked nonsense. Tsz Ching shouldn't have asked him all sorts of silly questions about the march and the tanks. The more he talked, the worse he got. He was completely carried away when you and Nathan joined us."

"So that was what you were talking about," said Margaret.

"Yes, but that was only a small part of it," said Cindy with a sigh. "If you had joined us earlier, you would have ignored them like I did."

"So you didn't join their discussion?" asked Margaret.

"No, of course not. Like you, I focused my attention on the guy I like."

"So, you like Alan?"

"Why not?" Cindy openly expressed her feelings. "He's a nice enough guy. I like his sense of humour." After a short pause, Cindy added, "He's very caring too."

"I think he also likes you."

"I am sure he does. Guess what? We've already exchanged our numbers. He said he's going to call me and fix a date."

"He was very direct," said Margaret with a blush. Suddenly, she wasn't sure if her comment was referring to Alan or Nathan, who was also very open with his feelings. Quickly, she turned to the locker and started rummaging as a way to hide her face.

"Maybe," said Cindy. "What happened to you and Nathan? How did everything go?"

"What about us? I don't know what you're talking about."

"Come on, you can't fool us. We all have eyes. We can all tell something's happened between the two of you. When you joined us again, you both looked different."

"Really? How did we look?"

"I'm not exactly sure. It was your face," said Cindy with some hesitation. "I think your face glowed, and so did Nathan's."

Before Margaret had time to comment on Cindy's observation, their conversation was cut short by Alan, who was calling their names from the corridor, urging them to hurry up. How Margaret welcomed such a timely interruption!

Margaret didn't quite enjoy her swim in this public pool. To her disappointment, nothing came close to what she had imagined. For one thing, she wasn't used to swimming in an indoor pool. The noise and the smell of chlorine was ever more intense in an enclosed environment. She found it hard to understand why people chose to swim indoors in the summer when they could enjoy the sun so much better in an outdoor pool or, even better, on the beach. Having a lane exclusive to their use (for Nathan belonged to a swimming club that booked two lanes every day from three to seven o'clock) only made her swimming experience marginally tolerable. Having their territory marked off by a divider was useful, but at the back of her mind, Margaret knew that all swimmers in the pool shared the same water that knew no boundary and flowed freely, whether she liked it or not.

Not being good at hiding her feelings, Margaret had her irritation written all over her face. She was even more annoyed to have Nathan swimming around her. Wasn't everyone supposed to be swimming laps in these two lanes? Why didn't Nathan let her swim but instead held her back every time she was about to start swimming her lap?

Another reason why she didn't enjoy her swim was because of Nathan's aggressive behaviour. He wasn't aggressive to her, only to anyone who tried to come close to Margaret. He was overly protective of his girlfriend, so much so that whenever

Margaret tried to swim a few paces away from him, he grabbed her back. He would let her swim for about ten to fifteen meters, then quickly overtake her on one side and then hold her waist with both hands. This hasty movement would allow him to swim alongside Margaret for a few paces before Nathan submerged his body into the water. He would then swim right underneath Margaret with his head almost touching her body. Margaret never liked being tickled, so she always stopped when Nathan started exhaling, making bubbles as though they stroked her stomach and her breasts. He did this a few times until Margaret lost control of her balance in the water. This was when she started choking and couldn't stop coughing until she turned crimson.

Margaret finally lost her temper. In between her gasps, she said, "Why did you do that?"

"To punish you," said Nathan.

"To punish me? Why?" asked Margaret.

"For coming here in a wrong swimming suit."

"What's wrong with it?" said Margaret in a slightly raised voice.

"Nobody wears bikini for training," Nathan retorted.

"I don't come here for training," said Margaret.

"You have to," said Nathan. "That's what these two lanes are reserved for."

"I can go and swim somewhere else," said Margaret, "if you don't like my swimwear."

Alan and Cindy came to their rescue before their argument became too heated. "What are you discussing?" asked Alan.

"Nothing," said Nathan, knowing that they must have already overheard their conversation. "Why are you not training my student?"

"I told you," said Alan with a frown, "she called in sick. You didn't listen to me, did you?"

"Oh, yes, you did. So why are you two not swimming?"

"We were," said Alan, "until we heard you argue."

"Shall we race the four of us, you and Margaret in a team, and me and Alan in this lane?" suggested Cindy, hoping that this would stop them quarreling.

"That's a good idea. I'll be the judge," came a voice from the edge of the pool.

They looked up to trace the voice and found Tsz Ching standing by the pool. When had she arrived? And how long had she been watching them?

"You came early," said Nathan. "Training starts in about twenty minutes."

"I know," said Tsz Ching. "I can't stay for long today. I figured if I came early, I could still train for half an hour or so. Can I leave early?"

"What's wrong with everyone?" Nathan found it convenient to air his anger at Tsz Ching, who seemed to have phrased her request too casually. "No one seems to be in the mood for practice."

"I am in the mood to compete," said Cindy. "Shall we start now?"

"If you like," said Nathan. "Don't cry when you lose."

"We won't lose," said Cindy. "Tell them we will win. Go on, Alan, tell them."

Under Tsz Ching's arrangement, they started the race without any more discussion. What could Alan say to Cindy when she made her challenge to one of the best swimmers in the city? They lost the race; they made a terrible showing as everyone watched Alan swim his last twenty meters.

"It doesn't count," said Cindy as soon as Alan reached the edge of the pool. "It doesn't count when the two of you are professionals."

"I'm not a professional," protested Margaret.

"But you can be one if you choose to," said Cindy. "You swim at your posh club with everyone so good at it. You can't lie to me. I went there with you once."

Ever since she was a kid, Margaret's parents had taken her to swim regularly at a club for expatriates and retired swimming athletes. That was where she had learned how to swim in the most proper and professional manner. She was fortunate to have learned from the experts. Unlike some of her classmates, including Cindy who learned how to swim in a haphazard way, Margaret did not pick up any bad habits.

"Some club members swim well, but not all of them. Don't you remember the posers and the sunbathers? There were lots of them."

On hearing Margaret's summary of the swimmers at the club, everyone except Tsz Ching responded immediately.

"I didn't know you learned swimming at a club," said Nathan.

"But you only socialise with the fast swimmers," said Cindy.

"Cindy's right. It's only fair that we have another race, and this time only for professionals," said Alan.

"That's right. Tsz Ching will pair up with Alan, and I'll be the judge," said Cindy, who was eager that Alan win the second race. "We will get even with them."

"That's not fair," said Nathan. "Margaret has never been trained for competitions. She doesn't have an athlete's muscles."

"How about this? You can all swim freestyle, and I'll swim the breaststroke," said Tsz Ching, who had kept quiet for a long time. "You know how lousy my breaststroke is, right?"

"Come on, Nathan. Don't be a coward." Cindy kept pressing him to accept the challenge. "See how eager everyone is about the race?"

They had surely drawn a large crowd of spectators. Among them were casual swimmers as well as caretakers who had brought children here for swimming lessons. Now that everyone was watching them so closely, how could Nathan withdraw from the race?

"I have a suggestion," said Tsz Ching.

"What is it?" asked Nathan.

"Let's swim two laps each, and this time the guys will go first."

"Why?' asked Alan. Not even her teammate understood the strategy.

"I have better stamina with distance than speed in breaststroke," said Tsz Ching as she cast a quick look at Nathan. "This will make it a much closer race, right?"

"Agreed," said Nathan.

"The losing team will treat everyone to a big meal," said Cindy.

"So, you are the sure winner," teased Alan.

"Of course," said Cindy. "I'm the judge, and you can't argue with me. Now, on your mark."

It was unusual not to save the best swimmers for the last lap in a relay race, but they were not having a serious race, were they?

To secure the championship as he always did, Nathan had his adrenalin going and swam the best he could. By the time Margaret jumped into the water, they were well ahead of their opponents.

Almost everyone had stopped swimming and was now watching this race. Most of the spectators knew Nathan, so they naturally cheered for him and Margaret; only a few, including the judge, were hoping that Alan and Tsz Ching would catch up.

When Margaret was swimming her last lap, she saw Tsz Ching coming in the opposite direction, trying her best to finish the first fifty meters. As they passed by one another in the middle of the pool, something happened in that split second. From where Nathan was, he couldn't quite make out why Margaret looked as though she lost her momentum in her swimming stroke. Clearly, she was trying her best to regain her balance by turning her head much higher and longer than normal, taking in a big breath. But nothing helped. First, Margaret gasped for air; she then stopped swimming completely, standing in the middle of the pool trying to catch her breath.

Everyone was disappointed to see the race come to a pause. People started moving about, turning their heads from the pool to the finishing line. As soon as Tsz Ching made a flip turn and started swimming back to where Margaret was, the spectators started shouting, "Stop the cramp."

Suddenly, everyone including Nathan was cheering for Margaret, chanting together, "Stop the cramp! Stop the cramp! Stop the cramp!"

As Tsz Ching was swimming close by and was about to overtake her, Margaret stretched out in the water again, first kicking her legs only, then moving her arms, doing the catch and the pull in the water before making a recovery. Margaret made this series of actions quite consciously and slowly in the beginning, as though she were having her first swimming lesson. She then picked up her speed and swam normally again. This was also the time the crowd started cheering again and chanted, "No more cramps! No more cramps! No more cramps!"

A few seconds made great distances in the pool, however. Seeing that Tsz Ching was already swimming well ahead of her, Margaret knew there was no way she could catch up, but she would finish the race anyhow.

The spectators who were not used to seeing any white girls swimming in their community pool couldn't keep their excited emotions under control. They all started chanting another phrase, "Go, Gweimui, go," again in Cantonese.

When she finally completed the swim and was pulled out of the water, Nathan held her tightly in his arms, checking to see if she was all right. Even when she assured him that there was nothing wrong with her, he was not convinced and wouldn't let go of her. If nobody was watching, Margaret knew this boyfriend of hers would first cry sadly before being all over her, kissing and stroking her until his tears dried.

"Are you sure you are okay?" asked Nathan.

"Absolutely," said Margaret. "But I can't wait for you. I am sorry I lost the race." Turning to Cindy, she continued, "I'm sorry, Cindy, I can't take you out for a meal today. I must go home now. Shall we eat another time?"

"No problem. Go home and rest," said Cindy. After announcing that Alan and Tsz Ching were winners of the race, she quickly went over to Nathan and Margaret, taking their hands in hers and raising them in the air to show that they were winners too.

"Here is the team that shows good sportsmanship," said Cindy before following the girls to the changing rooms.

Cindy was quarreling with Tsz Ching as Margaret emerged from a quick shower.

"Why did you do that?" said Cindy. "I've never seen such wicked behaviour."

"I don't know what you're talking about," said Tsz Ching.

"Do you think I'm blind?" said Cindy. "The guys are idiots, but I'm no fool. You can fool them, but not me."

Seeing that Margaret had come out from the shower, she asked, "Are you okay? It must hurt a lot."

"I'm fine, really. I just need to go home and rest," said Margaret.

"Do you mind if I take a look?" said Cindy as she was lifting her friend's towel. Margaret didn't respond but let Cindy lift her towel to reveal a nasty bruise in her upper thigh. It was a big patch of reddish green. "Oh my goodness! See what you've done."

"It was an accident," said Tsz Ching.

"It wasn't an accident," retorted Cindy. "You planned it. That was why you suggested swimming the breaststroke."

"That's not true," said Tsz Ching. "The lanes are narrow. Anyone who trains here knows we must keep right."

"I did," said Margaret in a feeble voice.

"Did you hear that?" said Cindy as she gently put her finger on the bruise.

It was certainly very painful. The moment Cindy touched the bruise, Margaret gave out a loud cry. Involuntarily, her towel dropped on the floor. However brief the moment was, Margaret clearly saw a pair of jealous eyes staring at her body. She felt extremely uneasy. "Why don't you stop arguing? I'm fine. I just need some rest."

"You must apologise to Margaret," said Cindy, "before she leaves."

"I'm not saying sorry to anyone. I didn't do anything wrong. I told you it was an accident," Tsz Ching said in an uncompromising tone.

Margaret had by this time cleared the locker and was walking out of the changing rooms. "See you in the Japanese class."

"Margaret," cried Cindy, "don't go yet. I'll make her say sorry to you."

"I won't. Don't even think about it."

"Do you think you have a choice?"

Margaret slipped away, for she was not bothered whether Tsz Ching had ill intentions when she gave her that brutal kick. She hoped that it was an accident, but subconsciously she knew it was a price she had to pay for being so attractive to Nathan. It was wise to leave now, or she might have to deal with another episode of rivalry.

AN EXPEDITION

Dominic's unexpected appearance at the entrance of the sports complex upset her plan to go home and rest.

"Hi, Dominic," greeted Margaret as she was walking in his direction. "Nathan is still training, but Cindy and Tsz Ching will finish their showers anytime now. They won't be long."

"I didn't come here for them," said Dominic. "I'm waiting for you."

"Me? Why?" Margaret couldn't help staring at Dominic with surprise.

"Come, I need your help. It's urgent," said Dominic. "We have no time to talk now. We've been waiting for too long."

"Who are you talking about?" asked Margaret.

Dominic kept his mouth shut on their way to somewhere that Margaret wasn't familiar with. As they were crossing the harbour tunnel in a bus, she tried to get him talk but to no avail. Dominic refused to communicate and had his eyes closed for almost the whole journey except to open them to check the time on his watch a few times.

At last, they got off in Yau Ma Tei, a district that Margaret only came to when visiting her retired nanny. She now lived a reasonably comfortable life in one of those low-rise old buildings on a pension provided by Margaret's parents. Every time they came to visit her nanny, her father drove, so she had no practical need to find her way around.

Dominic was walking fast, not exactly running, a few paces ahead of Margaret. They first passed by a basketball court where a few teenagers were playing, then a street market with hawkers selling food and daily necessities such as mirrors, nail clippers, and plastic containers, and finally a jade market.

Now, she was brought to a back street that gave off an eerie feeling. A bunch of guys, mostly middle-aged and some looked older, were standing in small groups. They clustered with their shoulders hunched and their heads down, seemingly looking intensely at something they were holding in their hands. Margaret had no idea who these men were and what they were doing, but the sight scared her. She quickly ran to catch up with Dominic. "Wait. Wait for me."

"Hurry up, we are already late," urged Dominic.

"Why are you bringing me here?" asked Margaret. No reply. "Who are those men?"

"Don't mind them. They won't hurt you," said Dominic.

"I don't like it. I'm leaving." Margaret stopped walking.

"Please, don't go away," said Dominic. "I need your help."

Those sinister-looking men stared at Margaret, and this sent shivers down her spine.

"Stop looking at them," Dominic quickly said. "If we keep walking, they'll ignore us."

As they were walking past these men, Margaret held onto Dominic, trying to hold her breath. Having walked a good distance, she asked, "Who were those men?"

"Drug addicts."

"What?" Margaret gave out a low cry, not wanting to attract any attention. "I'm going home. I don't like this area."

"I'm sorry," apologised Dominic. "I can't let you go. We've come this far. You must help me." It seemed as if Dominic was going to cry, but Margaret didn't understand why.

On seeing this, Margaret softened and continued walking with him. A minute later, they came to a street that seemed lively with noise and activities. Here, Dominic stuck his hand into a big backpack and took out a bagful of stuff.

"Now, take this and give it to the person inside." Margaret followed Dominic's eyes to check what he was referring to. She was shocked to see no other facilities than the public toilets.

"You want me to take this bag into the female toilets?" said Margaret in a puzzled voice.

Dominic nodded his head.

"No way," said Margaret. "I'm not smuggling drugs for you."

"There are no drugs inside," said Dominic. "You can take a look at it if you want to."

Margaret opened the bag a little to check its content. There was some bread, biscuits, and juice. She rummaged into it and found a few first-aid items like dressings, bandages, and cloth tape.

"Was someone hurt?" asked Margaret. "Why is she staying in the toilet?"

"My friend's in the last cubicle," said Dominic. "Please go now."

Not all her questions were answered, but for some reason Margaret suddenly felt a strong urge to assist Dominic with his mission. He was right. They had gone this far. If his friend needed help, she had to help her. His friend had to have her reason for remaining in the toilets. She was perhaps running away from her abusive parents.

In this late afternoon, everyone was busy going about their business. Nobody turned their heads to look at Margaret except a few women who were standing on the pavement, talking with each other after their grocery shopping. These onlookers were a little curious, but after a while, they lost interest in her actions. As instructed, she went inside the female toilets, towards the last cubicle, and knocked on the door. When nothing happened, Margaret knocked again and said, "I'm Margaret, a friend of Dominic. He asked me to bring you some food."

There was a slight pause before the door opened just wide enough for Margaret to slip in the plastic bag.

It wasn't long before Margaret heard the sounds of chewing and swallowing.

"Do you need help? Are you hurt?" Met with no reply, Margaret was getting a little angry. How rude his friend was! But Margaret gave her the benefit of the doubt and made a last attempt, "I'm going now. Do you have a message for Dominic?"

There was a complete silence; even the sound of munching stopped. Was she badly hurt?

"Are you okay?" Margaret was concerned.

"Yes."

As soon as Margaret heard the reply, she ran out of the toilets, screaming at the top of her voice at Dominic, "Why didn't you tell me your friend is a man?"

"I am sorry," said Dominic hurriedly. "Don't breathe a word to anyone. I'll call you later."

"Don't call me. I'm not talking to you anymore." Margaret was already running on the other side of the street, heading to the main road.

On her way to the bus stop, Margaret was thinking how incredibly crazy the last couple of days had been. When she yearned for something to happen in her life, she didn't expect her days to be so eventful. She had her first dance in a disco, her first kiss with a first-rate swimmer, and now her first delivery of food to a man hiding in a female toilet. What she considered a charitable act had suddenly turned into something ridiculous.

Wait, why was Dominic's friend hiding in a female toilet? Who would have been so crazy to consume food inside a smelly toilet? He had to have no choice. If he was a psychopath, he would have taken advantage of her innocence when she got close, but he did her no harm. So, what was going on?

It didn't take long before Margaret was overcome with sleepiness and dozed off on the bus as her tired body rocked back and forth. She was too tired to eat dinner and went straight to bed as soon as she unloaded her swimming gear. She slept through the night unexpectedly well.

DEPARTURE

A rather unusual sight made Margaret hesitate slightly as she walked out from her bedroom: Mom and Dad were having breakfast together. It was already nine o'clock, a time when her dad would usually be in his office.

"Morning," greeted Margaret as she poured herself a glass of orange juice.

"You slept for fourteen hours," said Betty.

"Did I? I was so tired after the swim," said Margaret.

"I want you to get changed as soon as we finish breakfast," ordered her mother.

"Where are we going?" asked Margaret.

"She wants to go and see our travel agent about changing the date of our departure," said her dad.

"Why?" asked Margaret. "Didn't we set to leave in early September?"

"I can't wait," said her mom. "I can't stand it anymore. Every day I turn on the tele there's nothing but reports about Tiananmen Square. And look at the protests in Hong Kong. The city is not safe anymore."

"There are no protests," said Margaret. "They are just peaceful marches."

"You call that peaceful? I got stuck in the traffic for more than an hour the other day," said her mom.

"So, when are we leaving?" asked Margaret.

"The next flight, as soon as the travel agent can find us three seats on our flight to Winnipeg. The tricky part is the connecting flight," said her mom.

"What? You mean anytime now?" screamed Margaret.

"I'm afraid so," said her dad.

"No, I can't leave so soon." Margaret was thinking of Nathan, Cindy, Dominic, and also his friend in the toilet.

"You don't have a choice, young lady," said her mom.

"I must stay to finish my Japanese course. I paid for my lessons until August."

"I told you to quit your Japanese course."

"What are we going to do with our apartment? We haven't cleared it yet."

"We're keeping this apartment," said her dad. "It is our base, and I'll stay here whenever I come back for my business. You can also stay here for your holidays."

"But I haven't said goodbye to my friends yet." As soon as Margaret said this, she started crying.

"Tut, look at her," said her mom. "What a crying baby!"

When Margaret finally managed to control herself, she said between her sobs, "I've known Cindy all my life. I can't leave without saying goodbye to her properly."

What Margaret said made a lot of sense to her father. He asked, "You mean organising a party or something like that?"

"No, not really," said Margaret. "What I meant was I need to spend time with her. Who knows when I will see her again? I did promise that we would be together the whole summer." Margaret would, of course, spend time with Nathan too, but she decided not to mention him at a time like now.

"Just tell her that you can't now," said Betty. "You can perhaps invite her to come and visit us in Canada." After a short pause, she added, "Only, I'm not sure if I can stand her high-pitched Cantonese and the way she laughs, but never mind, I'll bear it if that pleases you."

"Spending time with her in Hong Kong is different," said Margaret.

"Now, don't argue with me," said her mother, who was getting impatient.

"I'm not going," Margaret said, sulking. She then changed her attitude and suddenly became quite aggressive. "If you think you can make me leave now, you are wrong."

Knowing that there would soon be a deadlock between mother and daughter, her dad quickly said, "How about this? Mother and I will leave first. We need time to sort things out anyway. I think it will be much easier to rent a place, buy a car, and settle everything if there are just the two of us. I will then come back and collect you on my next business trip, which I think will be sometime in September. Will this do?"

"Who's going to look after her in Hong Kong?" asked Betty.

"I can take care of myself," said Margaret immediately, knowing that she would only win if she didn't give her mother time to think. "I will turn sixteen soon."

"That's right," said her dad. "Isn't this the reason why we are moving back to Canada? Margaret can learn to be independent by living here on her own. Don't worry, Jennifer will come and check on her every now and then."

"I'll be sensible, don't worry," said Margaret. "Please, please let me stay."

After a long while, her mother finally said, "Okay, you'd better be good."

"Thanks, Mom. You are wonderful." Margaret leaned over to hug and kiss her mother.

"Cut it out. I'll go and get changed," said her mother.

"I'll do the plates."

"I can still change my mind whether you do the plates or not."

"I know you won't," said Margaret with a smile.

When Margaret was alone with her father, she thanked him for talking her mother into this impossible agreement.

"I know how you feel," said her dad. "I find it a bit rushed too, but I can't argue with your mother, can I?" Before Margaret went back to her bedroom, her father lowered his voice and asked, "Who is Dominic?"

Margaret turned to look at her father and asked, "Did he call?"

"Yes, last night at about eight. I told him that you were sleeping, and he thanked me. He sounded rather polite."

"Did he leave a message?"

"No, but he asked you to phone him as soon as you can." Her father then added after a short pause, "He said it's important." Not getting a reply from his daughter, he asked, "Is he your boyfriend?"

"No," said Margaret with a laugh. "I'll call him after we finish the ticketing business. Thanks."

"Okay," said her father.

"Okay? You mean you are not asking any more questions about this Dominic?" asked Margaret.

"No. Why would I if you don't want to tell me anything now?" said her father.

"You do trust me, don't you?" asked Margaret. If it had been her mother who answered the phone call, it would have been completely different. She would now have been pestering Margaret for all the details. "What would you say if I told you I have a boyfriend?"

"So, do you?" asked her father.

"Yes, I do, but it's not Dominic," replied Margaret softly. "Will you still let me stay in Hong Kong on my own now that you know I have a boyfriend?"

Rather than answering her question, he asked, "Who is your boyfriend? What is his name?"

"His name is Nathan," said Margaret. "He's a champion swimmer."

"Where did you meet him?" asked her father.

"Through a girlfriend I met in the Japanese class," said Margaret. "Please don't tell Mom."

"No, I won't; don't worry."

"Will you still let me stay in Hong Kong on my own?"

"Why not?"

"Oh, that's great." Margaret could neither believe her ears nor conceal her excitement. "Thank you for trusting me."

"I know you are sensible, like me," said her father with an encouraging smile. "Well, that's only partly true. The truth is, I have always had a soft spot for you. I'll do anything to make you happy. You are always my darling girl."

Margaret leaned over to hug her father. It was so tight that they almost fell together on the floor. "Thanks, Dad!"

"Do you have one?" asked her father.

"What, a soft spot?" Margaret wasn't sure if she understood her father.

"Yes," said her father. "Would it be Nathan?"

"I don't know," said Margaret. After a while, she added, "No, I don't think so, at least not for now. How about Mom? Does she have one?"

"I'm not sure if she does," said her father. "Maybe it's her birthplace."

Their conversation was cut short by an impatient voice. "I thought the two of you would be ready by now."

***

Changing the date of departure on the plane tickets didn't take long. In fact, it wasn't long before Margaret's parents flew out of Hong Kong. Margaret and her aunt Jennifer saw them off at the Kai Tak Airport. As she was waving them goodbye, Margaret promised that she would be good and would call her aunt every day. Jennifer, who was only eight years older than Margaret, was her father's youngest sibling. There was almost no hope that this liberal-minded auntie would be strict to her niece, but nobody seemed to be too concerned about leaving a fifteen-year-old girl behind. Even Margaret's mother wasn't too worried. Her priority was to get out of Hong Kong without having to listen to the reports about the student activists. One thing Betty couldn't quite work out was why her daughter insisted on staying in Hong Kong. Was it so important to complete a Japanese course? Why was Margaret so stubborn and insisting on finishing off something? It was perhaps a Chinese trait that mother and daughter didn't share with one another.

Enjoying her new freedom, Margaret went out with Nathan every day. Other than his training sessions, they spent all their time together. They would go bowling, dancing, eating, and watching films, sometimes with Cindy and Alan, but mostly on their own. Of all these activities, Margaret enjoyed going to the movies because Nathan would always let her choose her favourite, except the time when Margaret wanted to see a thriller. Nathan tried to change her mind, saying that this kind of film was too bloody and unsuitable for the faint-hearted. "Definitely not for girls," Margaret remembered him saying this as they were about to choose their seats. It turned out that it wasn't Margaret but Nathan who got so scared that he kept screaming every time the serial killer was about to attack the next victim. If it had not been for those cold, sweaty hands, Margaret would have thought Nathan was pulling her leg. How would she expect him to be genuinely afraid?

"I need something sweet to calm my nerves," whispered Nathan in her ear.

"We can go for an ice-cream after the film," said Margaret.

"No, I need something much sweeter," whispered Nathan again. "I want you to cook for me."

"I don't use much sugar in my cooking. It can't be very sweet," said Margaret.

"I meant it figuratively, silly girl." Nathan held Margaret's hand to his lips and kissed it several times before cupping it in his big hands.

"I'll need to call Jennifer to make sure she's not around," said Margaret.

"Who is Jennifer?"

"My aunt," said Margaret. "Remember? I told you about her before. She's supposed to keep an eye on me for my parents."

Their conversation was cut short as the person sitting in front of them turned round to show his annoyance.

As soon as the film was over, Nathan urged Margaret to check on her aunt, who said over the phone that she was too busy to have dinner with her. On hearing this, Nathan quickened his steps, leading their way to a supermarket nearby. He was getting rather impatient when Margaret was choosing her ingredients.

"Anything will do. We are not having a feast." There was a sense of urgency in Nathan's voice. "I'm starving."

They left in such a hurry that they didn't even take the change from the cashier.

"I didn't know you were so hungry," said Margaret as soon as they arrived home. "We could have stopped for a snack."

She was just beginning to arrange the grocery shopping when Nathan came close to her, holding her very tightly in his arms. "Oh, Margaret, how I love you," he said as he put his lips on her hair. "What am I going to do when you're gone? How am I going to live?"

It turned out that Nathan's hunger was of a different kind. At that moment, he suddenly decided on a whim that he would spend the rest of his life with Margaret. He was neither interested in his swimming career nor his future anymore. He didn't mind giving up on everything in order that they could be together.

"Don't leave," Nathan whispered into Margaret's ear, pleading. "Stay in Hong Kong and stay with me."

Before Margaret had time to respond, Nathan was already on his knees holding her legs with both hands. To Margaret's surprise, he started crying. "Please don't leave me. I can't bear to lose you."

"I'm not leaving yet," said Margaret. "Get up, please." Not getting a response, Margaret became a little impatient and said in a firm voice, "Get up now."

This time, Nathan did respond by looking Margaret in the eyes as though he were peering into her soul. Before she knew it, he was kissing her legs. She found his touch ticklish and was trying very hard not to giggle, for she found Nathan's behaviour laughable and senseless. She couldn't understand how his outburst of tears suddenly disappeared without a trace. The transformation from a state of despair to that of passion and intimacy was incredible.

But Margaret also felt sorry and helpless for not being able to stop his anguish or share his sentiments. Although she wished she were staying in Hong Kong, Nathan was only part of the reason. She enjoyed her newfound freedom and the time she spent with all her friends so much that it made her wonder if she would still have a jolly good time without a boyfriend. In the last few weeks, she had tried many new things for the first time in her life: bowling, playing snooker, drinking, and dancing. Even though these were quite normal activities for young people, Margaret's mother wouldn't have approved. Bowling alleys, bars, and discos were nothing but places filled with smoke and coarse language. Betty couldn't understand why young people were drawn to them.

As she smiled to herself for having carried out all these naughty acts without her mother knowing it, she started ruffling his hair, keeping her hands in pace with her own heartbeat. It was a lovely moment, one that reminded her of their first dance. Margaret really enjoyed the peace and quiet of her home. Other than her neighbour playing Bach's preludes and fugues on the piano, Margaret heard no other noise.

For some reason, the ticklish feeling was now gone. She could feel Nathan's soft touch on her thighs, the warmth of his palms seeping through the silky fabric of her one-piece summer dress. As Nathan drew his lips close to her belly button, Margaret felt as if her body were electrified. Both time and space were of no significance any longer. She was just standing there, fixated on that same spot next to the fridge while Nathan knelt in front of her for who knows how long. It was an important moment in Margaret's life. It was her first experience of being wanted as a woman.

Just when she was immersing herself in this moment of eternity, something happened that really scared her. She noticed her hands that were still ruffling Nathan's hair were moving upwards, getting close to her bosom. Now, both her own breathing and that of Nathan's quickened. By this time, her neighbour had stopped playing Bach. With no music in the background, she could only hear their own breathing. Rather than those beautiful colours and patterns that filled her mind's eye a moment ago, her eyes were now confronted with a strange male body that she couldn't register. Margaret pushed it away and said decisively, "Stop."

Nathan looked up at her, not knowing what she meant. As he was about to kiss her again, Margaret repeated her request. "I said stop." She then added, "Please."

Unlike his other girlfriends, this was a voice full of power and determination. Margaret might appear soft and fragile, but she could stand up for herself if she chose to.

When Nathan finally registered the meaning of her words, he opened the fridge and poured himself a cold drink. After drinking half of it in one gulp, he said, "I'm sorry."

A big childish grin on Nathan's face softened Margaret, and she let him hold her hands again. The two of them sat on the sofa; neither of them knew whether they should talk about what had happened or just leave it like that. They were both embarrassed to have experienced a moment of intimacy, not knowing how to deal with it. Having experienced one another's bodies, their relationship was not quite the same. It would never be the same.

This uneasy silence broke when the telephone rang. Margaret ran to answer it, for she was eager for some interruption from the outside world. Nathan couldn't make out of what she said over the phone because Margaret had lowered her voice. Only when she said, "No, you can't," did he come over to check on her.

Margaret signaled that everything was okay and continued with her telephone conversation. "I've bought some food. If you are tired, I can cook something for you," said Margaret in a rather helpless manner.

"Who was that?" asked Nathan as soon as Margaret put down the phone.

"It was my aunt," Margaret lied. "She changed her mind. She's just finished her work in the office and wants to come and see me now."

"Then I'd better leave," said Nathan. "I don't suppose you want us to meet."

"No, you'd better leave."

In a way, they were both relieved at not having to talk about their relationship for the moment. Seeing that Margaret was occupied with thoughts, Nathan was concerned. "I hope you are not upset about what I did."

"No, I'm not. Don't worry," said Margaret. "I'll see you tomorrow. You'd better go now, or you'll bump into my aunt."

"Okay, I'll see you tomorrow," Nathan quickly planted a kiss on Margaret's mouth. As he was about to leave, he turned round and asked, "You spoke to your aunt in Cantonese just now. I wonder why."

"Oh, I speak to her in both Cantonese and English," said Margaret. "We switch as we feel like it."

"I see," said Nathan. "Enjoy your dinner with your aunt. Bye."

Margaret was surprised at her own ready wit. As soon as Nathan left, she started wondering if it was wise to let her boyfriend go. Having freed herself from the company of a male friend, she was going to let another one in. But the thing was when she picked up the receiver and heard Dominic's voice on the other end, she was curious to find out why he called. They hadn't met after the public-toilet incident, but she hadn't stopped thinking about what Dominic was up to.

So, when she received his phone call, she somehow felt happy and excited. It was as though she would encounter another new experience. Not that she already got tired of Nathan. Why would she when they were so madly in love with each other? Margaret just wanted something . . . different. She wanted to find out more about the person she met in the public toilet. All she had to do was talk nicely to Dominic, and he would surely tell her everything.

Margaret did not end up asking a single question about his friend. She didn't have to. Dominic brought his friend along, who did not open his mouth except for the time when he ate. Her knowledge of this person hadn't moved up a notch even after eating a meal together. How frustrating it was when she didn't even manage to make Dominic speak! Silence seemed to be a disease spreading over the dining table. Without talking or making eye contact, the two young men kept eating the spaghetti Bolognese that Margaret had intended to cook for Nathan.

Margaret finally lost her temper when neither of them showed any intention of making a conversation or a departure.

"I think you'd better leave now that dinner is over," said Margaret with annoyance.

Either because Margaret didn't use a very harsh tone, or Dominic was too dumb to pick up any traces of anger in her voice, he said matter-of-factly, "My friend is staying here for the night."

"What?" Margaret exclaimed. "You're staying? You must be mad."

"Only my friend, not me."

Now Margaret was getting really furious, "No one can stay here. I don't even let my boyfriend stay overnight. What makes you think you can just bring your friend here to eat and sleep for free?"

"I'm really sorry," said Dominic, "but I don't know who we can turn to. Can you just let him stay here for one night? I promise he will leave tomorrow."

"Why isn't he going home?" asked Margaret.

"He can't." After a pause, Dominic added, "It's not safe for him. He has trouble with his family." Dominic then turned to look at his friend and said, "You're having trouble with your family, right?"

It's the first time Margaret had a good look at his friend. Sitting at the far end of the long dining table was this young man in a plain T-shirt that had turned from cream to dirty grey. The two colours formed an interesting pattern after years of sweat and wash. His bushy eyebrows and high cheekbones made his eyes very prominent. His distinct features did not make him look like a local boy though. How old would he be? Eighteen, twenty, or twenty-one? The pale and sickly appearance aside, he was actually quite good-looking. There did not seem to be any colour on his cheekbones or his hands.

For the first time, his friend nodded his head and said, "Yes."

"I don't care if he has a family problem," said Margaret. "Why can't he stay with you?"

"I don't want my family to get involved," said Dominic.

"Oh, that's a good one, so you don't want your family to get involved, but you want me to get involved. How fair is that?" Margaret sneered.

"Please, could you help? I know your parents have moved to Canada," said Dominic.

"So, you've been checking on me. I can't believe it," said Margaret.

"Please don't get angry with me. I have no other choice," said Dominic. There was somehow a note of sadness in his voice that Margaret found hard to ignore. She knew how ridiculous it would be for her to comply with this request, yet she didn't have the heart to reject him.

As a father's girl, Margaret tried to imagine what her father would do. When she pleaded to stay in Hong Kong on her own, her father agreed readily. Didn't he say he didn't have the heart to turn her down? Was it the same for her now? Dominic had to be extremely desperate to turn to her for help. Could she not grant it without asking any more questions? She felt sorry that Dominic always appeared to be in a melancholy mood when she and her friends were enjoying themselves.

She said at last, "All right, I'll let him stay, only for one night, and on the condition that he won't get close to my bedroom."

"Oh, thank you. Thank you for being so kind to us," said Dominic. Turning to his friend, he said, "You will be good, and you will behave yourself, right?"

"Yes," said his friend.

"Where will he sleep?" asked Margaret. She didn't want him to sleep in her parents' room or the study where her father kept all his important documents.

"He could sleep on the floor in the living room. Just give him a throw or something," said Dominic. He again turned and checked with his friend. "You don't mind, do you?"

His friend shook his head with tears in his eyes.

Margaret had no idea why his friend appeared so emotional all of a sudden. *Maybe he is thinking of his family problems*, she thought. The way he cried was different from Nathan though. Rather than sobbing or letting his tears roll down, he blinked back his tears and managed to roll them back into his eyes, which were now staring at the floor.

When Margaret came out from the storeroom with a blanket, both Dominic and his friend were still standing where they were before. She handed the blanket to his friend and said, "Take this. It can get quite chilly at nighttime, particularly with the balcony door open. Just let me know if you need anything before I go to sleep," said Margaret. "I usually get up at eight."

"Oh, thanks, Margaret. I think he'll be fine," said Dominic. "You will be fine, right?"

Getting tired of speaking to his friend through Dominic, Margaret showed her annoyance. "Why can't you let him speak for himself?"

"Oh, sorry. I didn't mean to be bossy," said Dominic. "It's only because my friend is not very sociable."

"All right. I won't insist if your friend doesn't feel like talking," said Margaret. Before she walked back to her bedroom, she added, "Aren't you leaving yet?"

"I'll stay for a while and settle my friend, if you don't mind," said Dominic. "I will switch off the lights and close the door quietly when I leave." He added after a pause, "Is that okay?"

"Okay. Remember, no wild parties," said Margaret jokingly.

Slipping into her nightgown after the shower, all was quiet. No light came through the slits of the door that served as a divider between the living and the sleeping areas. Dominic must have left. What a day! She couldn't believe how much she had grown up in just one day. Margaret was mistress of both her body and her home, giving orders as she wished.

She had always been told how soft her skin was, but her experience of its magic on another person was the first of its kind when she witnessed how Nathan reacted upon touching her. Trying to recall what happened earlier today, Margaret retraced the path where Nathan's hands had been. She remembered his movements and started directing her fingers to make the same. Feeling the soft and supple touch under her fingertips, she began to understand what a great sensation it was. Her consciousness was gradually diminishing as her fingers moved further upward until they reached the waist and beyond. There was no background music this time, but all the same, she felt as if she were dancing in her room with her head turning at the rhythm of some unheard music.

When the memory path came to an end, Margaret could remember no more. She stopped at the same spot where Nathan's hand had been. Margaret finally came to her senses and opened her eyes with disbelief and great embarrassment. It was fortunate that nobody saw her. She had locked herself in her own bedroom, well protected from the outside world that was still oblivious to her yearning for womanhood.

It had to be the imaginary dance that made Margaret feel so hot and tired. She suddenly found it hard to bear the stifling air in the room and went over to open all the windows to their fullest. Rather than a breeze, she heard a murmur of male voices coming from the direction of the balcony. So, Dominic hadn't left, and he was still chatting to his friend who was said to be "not very sociable." Margaret had warned them of a change in temperature on the balcony, but she didn't tell them how close it was to her bedroom. From where she was, and because of the unusual layout of her apartment, she could see and almost hear everything in the balcony, yet no one was aware of her watchful eyes.

Not that Margaret wanted to spy on Dominic and his friend, but she could almost hear everything they said. If only they spoke a little louder. They had to be either talking in a very low voice, or they were whispering to one another. Margaret wondered what secrets they were sharing. She was so exhausted that she couldn't think anymore. With her eyelids getting heavier, she struggled to open them one more time as she noticed they were speaking in Mandarin. Her discovery came too briefly and too late. Her breathing turned heavy, and her mind went blank with sleep.

***

It was a good night's sleep. When Margaret woke up, it was already nine. She quickly changed into a T-shirt and a pair of jeans before stepping into the living room to check on her guest. *Why is it so quiet? Is he still asleep?*

It didn't take long before Margaret concluded that her guest had left. On the floor of the balcony was the blanket she gave him and two cushions that were usually placed on the two-seater. So, the guys must have used them either as pillows or padded seaters. *What time did they leave, and did they leave together? Did they talk overnight on the balcony?*

Margaret was hoping to have her questions answered when she saw a slip of paper on the dining table but was disappointed to find only a brief note of thanks. How rude! They didn't even stay a little longer to thank her in person. Oh well, she should at least be pleased to have the rest of the day for herself.

The phone rang in a way that Margaret could somehow guess who the caller was.

"Hello, what can I do for you?" said Margaret in a sexy voice.

"You can do a lot for me, but for the moment I just want to have breakfast with you," came the reply from the other end.

"I'll think about it. Why don't you call back in an hour?"

"What? An hour? No, I can't wait. I'll eat by myself."

"I don't think you'll have breakfast without me." Margaret started laughing.

"Why can't you be nice? I'm really starving." After a pause, Nathan added, "You must be hungry too . . . unless you had a big dinner with your aunt last night?"

A guilty feeling for having lied to her boyfriend started to develop. Margaret quickly said, "See you in our café in about half an hour. Will that do?"

"Absolutely."

The little coffee shop was in the same area where Nathan went for his training. After a few visits, it became their regular hang-out place. They spent so much time there that the owner treated them as friends and called them by their first names. In return, Margaret and Nathan did their best to find out everything about the café, including its history, and called it "our café." The owner was a young man in his late twenties. Five years ago, when he returned from Canada with a university degree, he fought hard against his family's disapproval of opening the coffee shop. When everyone thought that he should work in a bank, he insisted on working on his dream project. The first two years were extremely challenging. He couldn't afford taking on any staff and did everything himself. He had to learn to brew a nice cup of coffee using his own roasted coffee beans too. Being close to the sports complex helped the business. More and more young people started to seek out the place by word of mouth. Margaret enjoyed listening to his story and was planning that one day she would come back and build her career in Hong Kong.

"Will you come back?" asked Nathan as he was sipping his iced coffee from a straw in a tall glass.

"Sure, I'll come back, open a shop, and make it successful like this one," said Margaret.

"I don't mean that. I mean will you come back and spend time with me every summer?" asked Nathan.

"Of course," said Margaret. "We will spend every summer together. Either I come back to Hong Kong, or you will go and visit me in Canada."

"Are you planning your next summer again?" asked the coffee shop owner who had heard their discussion so many times before.

"You bet. Did you come home for your summer holiday when you were studying in Canada?" asked Nathan.

"No, I didn't."

"Why not? Did you not miss your family?" asked Margaret.

"For one thing, air tickets were too expensive for me. I was a poor student. My family couldn't afford it. Besides, I was going out with a girl from Malaysia at that time. We couldn't decide if we should spend our summer in Hong Kong or in her hometown," said the owner.

"What has happened to your girlfriend?" asked Margaret.

"I don't know. She's not my girlfriend anymore," said the owner. "I suppose we were not very serious about our relationship. We felt lonely living in a foreign country, and we just wanted some company."

"Oh, I'm sorry to hear it," said Margaret.

"There's nothing to be sorry about. It's part of growing up. It's part of life. Different people are obsessed with different things as we are growing up. Young people can lose themselves in different things like drugs, sex, alcohol, religion, you name it. It so happens that I am a little lost in relationships."

"Do you mean cross-cultural relationships?" asked Margaret.

"No, my issue is relationships with women," said the owner.

Margaret wanted to ask more, but Nathan became impatient with the conversation and chipped in, "Now, you must promise me that you will not feel lonely." Then he corrected his illogical reasoning. "I mean you must promise me not to get a boyfriend just because you feel lonely."

"So I can get a boyfriend for any reason other than feeling lonely?" teased Margaret.

"Don't you dare. I'll make you feel sorry," said Nathan in a threatening tone.

"Oh, look who's jealous," Margaret said as she was wagging her finger in front of Nathan.

Before Nathan lost his temper, the owner managed to stop the drama by announcing their second drink on the house.

"Hurray!" cheered Margaret and went over to give the owner a big hug. Taking the signal from her boyfriend, she quickly came back to their table and kissed Nathan first on his cheek, then his lips, all under his directions.

Margaret happily forgot everything about Dominic and his friend on the following few days when she and Nathan became almost the same person. They ate the same food, watched the same films, and used the same slang expressions. How could they resist not imitating one another when they spent so much time together?

They would have spent the rest of their summer like that if Nathan did not have to train for his first international competition. He'd trained so hard to earn this qualification that he didn't want to miss the chance. Nathan was well aware of the need for more intensive and rigorous training. Reluctantly, they now had to bear occasional separations that ranged from a few hours to a couple of days. During those times, Margaret usually stayed home and listened to music or went shopping with Cindy.

On a late afternoon when Margaret had made no social plans, she did not expect to receive a fateful phone call. Making and receiving phone calls was almost her natural instinct. Only when she looked back later in life did she realise how significant this one was.

When the phone rang, she ruled out the possibility of hearing Nathan's voice, knowing that he was still having his punishing training at the time. *The phone usually doesn't ring at this hour. Who would it be? Cindy or my aunt? I hope it is not Tsz Ching. She's stopped talking to me since Nathan and I go steady. What a shame!* Despite her brief mental preparation, Margaret was nevertheless caught by surprise on hearing a male voice.

"Where have you been? I've been calling you the last few days," said the caller.

"Who is this?" asked Margaret.

"It's Dominic. I have no time to chit-chat. Get yourself a pen and a piece of paper. I want you to write down an address."

Margaret did as she was told. When she finished writing down the address, she asked, "Is this a complete address, 134 Queen's Road West? Which floor?"

"Just put down the third floor," said Dominic.

"Why are you giving me this address? Whose address is it?" asked Margaret.

"It's mine. I want you to come and help me now."

"Help you with what?"

"I can't tell you over the phone. I'll tell you when you are here."

"I won't come unless you tell me what's going on. I don't like you dragging me into your secret world without telling me anything about it."

"I am sorry, but I really need your help. I promise this will be the last time."

"I'm not sure if I like it. You've been acting weird lately," said Margaret.

"It won't be long. All I need is for you to spare an hour. That's all, but your help means a lot to me. Please," Dominic said in a begging voice.

"Okay, I'll help you for the last time. From then on, I won't have anything to do with your funny business," said Margaret finally.

"Oh, thank you. Please come as soon as you can," said Dominic before he hung up.

Margaret was indeed being dragged into another world that was foreign to her. She could have rejected it, but it all began with her curiosity. She couldn't resist the urge of finding out what Dominic was hiding. *He has to be keeping a big secret. What is it?* Margaret was determined to get to the bottom of it.

What Margaret found intriguing was not only Dominic's behaviour, but also his friend's. She was almost sure that she would find them together. To ease her curious mind, she had no other choice and agreed to go along with their plan. It wasn't long before Margaret received another phone call from Dominic, telling her a change of plan. Rather than meeting him at his home, Margaret was now instructed to meet him at a pier in Kennedy Town at ten o'clock.

"Why so late? And where is this pier?" asked Margaret.

Ignoring her first question, Dominic made a brief reply. "Just walk along the waterfront. Don't go to the main pier. Walk to the left and you'll see another pier for cargo."

"What do you want me to go there for?" asked Margaret.

"To meet me and my friend," said Dominic.

"And then?" prompted Margaret.

"I'll tell you what to do later. Oh, I nearly forgot. Put on a plain T-shirt and jeans, something that doesn't look expensive. I'll see you later, okay?"

Dominic hung up before Margaret had time to change her mind. When she tried to contact him again, he did not pick up the call.

So, what could Margaret do now? Although she didn't like unfinished business and would always complete whatever she had at hand, this time was different. Dominic's requests were getting more and more ridiculous. What would her father have said if he knew about this? Would he let her help Dominic because she had promised to do so, or would he think it's stupid to offer help when she did not know what she would get herself into? Having observed how her father handled his business for years, she knew that he would comply with the request, no matter how unreasonable it might appear. In a world of business, relationships came first. The way to maintain them was to offer help when it was most needed. Her father's business partners always remembered his gestures of kindness. Without realising that it was her business mind that made the decision, it didn't take her long to stop agonising over the matter. When she left home, Margaret was convinced that she was doing the right thing.

Margaret would never forget what happened that night. She had never seen people make a heartbroken farewell. Seeing her friends and family off at the airport was a common scene, and it meant nothing but a few hours of eating and chatting at the departure hall. People came and went. Nobody would ever settle in a place for good, at least not the ones in Margaret's family and social circles. It didn't occur to Margaret that people would say goodbye to one another for good.

Margaret arrived in Kennedy Town at ten o'clock sharp. As she was walking along the waterfront, she kept looking out for Dominic and his friend. The streets were getting quieter as she was walking away from the residential area. A few people were still lingering around the main pier, smoking and chatting with one another. Margaret remembered the instructions and started walking away from the main pier. In the distance she could see some containers resting on barges anchored at another pier further on her left. It had to be half a kilometre before she reached the destination where her friends were supposed to be.

What's wrong with Dominic? Why can't we meet at the main pier? Damn! Margaret was cursing her friend when she heard a soft whistle. At first she thought she heard it wrong, but then it came again a few more times. Margaret backtracked a few steps so that she could hear better.

"This way." It was clearly Dominic's voice, although Margaret couldn't see him or his friend. Well away from the main pier, streetlamps were few and far between, so Margaret found it difficult to make out her surroundings.

"This way, come over here," came Dominic's voice again.

"Where are you? I can't see you." Margaret was getting impatient.

"Over here behind the newspaper stand."

Margaret looked to her right and, sure enough, there was a newspaper stand, well covered and securely locked for the night. As she walked towards the stand, two figures slowly emerged somewhere from the background. When they finally came into sight, she was surprised to see Dominic's friend first. Almost taller than Dominic by a head, he was about the same height as Margaret. Looking at him at eye level, Margaret was met with a bony and angular face of prominent and symmetrical features. Despite a slight sign of fatigue, he seemed to be in better spirits than before. His face was cleanly-shaven, and he had put on a different T-shirt.

"Hold her hand," said Dominic in an urgent tone.

Before Margaret realised what was happening, Dominic's friend was holding her hand very tightly. No matter how much she wanted to free her hand, she couldn't take it back from his grip.

"Let go of my hand. You're hurting me," cried Margaret.

"I'm sorry," said Dominic. "The two of you will be holding hands until we reach the pier."

"Why?" asked Margaret.

"Because this is the best way," said Dominic.

"To do what?" Margaret was unsure of his plan.

"To avoid any unnecessary suspicion," said Dominic.

"From whom?"

Margaret had to control herself before she lost patience. She was getting tired of talking to Dominic, who gave her so little information even when he was pressed. Turning to his friend, she said in a warning tone, "I'll scream if you don't loosen your grip. I mean it."

"Yang, please be nice to Margaret. We need her help," said Dominic to his friend in Mandarin. Now facing Margaret, he continued to say, but in Cantonese this time, "What I am telling you is important. I hope you won't breathe a word to anyone.

Tonight is crucial. We've planned it for so long, and we asked so many favours that I don't think there's going to be a second chance. Whether Yang can leave Hong Kong safely depends on you. So, from this moment until he boards, you are his cover. And the best way is for you to act as his girlfriend."

Seeing that Margaret was about to question him, he signaled her to wait. "I'm really sorry for dragging you into this. I owe you this big favour for life."

Dominic was getting emotional and had to pause for a while. Neither Margaret nor Yang said anything. They just waited for Dominic to collect himself.

When he spoke again, he sounded quite different and became rather upbeat. He now only focused on strategies. "So, the two of you will walk together like lovers. I'll be walking behind you, like a little brother. If we get into trouble, we'll let Margaret speak. Margaret, remember to speak in English and pretend that you don't understand Cantonese. No matter what, don't respond to anyone who speaks Cantonese to you. Remember that."

"Why?" asked Margaret.

"Because as long as you speak English, they will leave us alone," said Dominic.

"Who will leave us alone?" asked Margaret.

"The police."

Without giving her a chance to ask any questions, Dominic put Margaret's hand into Yang's.

Unlike the main pier, this one was not built for passengers and had boarding gangways that were appropriate only for cargo. Margaret had no idea which boat Yang would board and where it would take him. In a way, she was happy to share their secret even though it meant that she had to bear certain risks. But wasn't it what she had hoped for, an exciting summer?

They had now been waiting for an hour, and still not a single soul was in sight.

"When will the ship come?" asked Margaret.

"Anytime soon," said Dominic. "By the way, it'll be a speedboat, not a ship." As soon as he said that, he saw someone walking towards them from the corner of his eye. "Yang, put on your hood, quickly now."

"What are you doing here?" asked one of the two policemen.

Dominic signaled Margaret to speak, and she did so without any trouble. She was a member of the drama club at school, and one of her talents was to improvise.

"Nothing, just chatting," said Margaret.

The two policemen were both caught by surprise to hear English in this area, which was a predominantly local community.

After thinking for a while, the one with more stripes on his shoulder than the other one said, "So late?"

"What can I do? My family is going back to Canada soon, and I can't bring my boyfriend with me." Margaret moved closer to Yang, putting her arm into his as she gave her reply. "Don't worry, my boyfriend's mother sent his little brother to look after us." Turning to Dominic, Margaret said, "You will look after us, won't you?"

"Sure," said Dominic in his heavily accented English.

"Go home. You get trouble," said the same policeman.

"We will be good, and we'll just stay for a little longer, and then they will see me home."

"Where do you live?"

"MacDonnell Road," said Margaret.

"What about the two of you? Where do you live?"

"Queen's Road West," said Dominic.

"Both areas are quite far from here," said the other policeman in Cantonese.

Nobody responded, so the one with more stripes on his uniform had to speak again, "Taxi?"

"No, I think we can walk back," said Margaret. "In fact, we walked here without knowing that we've walked so far. Anyway, we'll be heading back soon," Margaret threw back her hair and smiled at them.

The two policemen looked at one another without knowing what to say. Finally, the one with more stripes said "Okay" before they both walked away.

Dominic knew that things would be a lot easier with Margaret around, but he hadn't expected it to be so easy.

About ten minutes after the police had left, a man approached them and said, "I'm looking for Yang."

"Here I am."

"Come with me," said the man. Then, turning to Margaret and Dominic, he said, "What are you doing here? You can't come along."

"I only want to say goodbye to my friend," said Dominic.

"If you want to say goodbye, do it here. I only take him," said the human smuggler.

"Is my friend's boat leaving at this pier?" asked Dominic.

"No, and don't ask any more questions. If he doesn't want to leave, I'm going now."

"He's leaving. Just give us a minute," said Dominic.

Margaret now spoke to the human smuggler in Cantonese, trying her best to engage him in a conversation so that he wouldn't get impatient. Meanwhile, Dominic and Yang talked to each other in low voices at a distance. When they were done, their eyes were all red. They shook hands for the last time, looking into each other's eyes without saying anything else.

"Let's go before the police come back. I should have finished my work half an hour ago," said the man, who must have been waiting for the police to leave before he showed himself.

Yang followed the man, walking with him to the far end of the waterfront. Before they turned into a bend of the promenade, Yang waved at Dominic for the last time. The two figures were now diminishing in size until they became two dots that receded into the distance. Margaret could see them no more.

"He's gone. I will never see him again." Dominic broke down into tears and got stuck with his words.

"Why? Where is he going?" asked Margaret.

Either because he was too absorbed with sadness or Margaret spoke too softly, Dominic ignored her questions and gave no reply.

***

This farewell scene was unexpectedly a rehearsal of another one that came a month later when Margaret flew back to Canada with her father. Changing her role as an observer to a leading one wasn't fun. No, not at all. It was all right to be there to witness how sad Dominic was to see his friend off, but to act out a similar scene herself was different. Even for someone good at acting like she was, it was hard to wear the right expression on her face. She was too young to be the centre of attention.

When her father asked "Are you ready?" on their way to the airport, she wasn't sure of her reply and said, "I think so."

"What do you mean by I think so?" asked her father.

"I dunno. I mean I always knew I would be leaving Hong Kong one day, but when the day arrives, I just feel so weird. I don't feel myself," said Margaret.

"You'll get over it soon," said her father. "There will be so many new things waiting for you in Canada. I bet you won't have much time to miss Hong Kong. By the way, will your boyfriend come to see you off?"

"He'd better come," said Margaret. "I want you to meet him. I've been wanting you to meet him for a long time. Too bad that you didn't come back earlier. We could've spent some time together. Never mind, he'll come and see me soon. When he comes to visit us in Canada next summer, can he stay in our place?"

"Sure, why not?"

When they arrived at the airport, a few relatives including her aunt Jennifer were already there. Because they chose to depart on a weekday in early September when the new term already started in Hong Kong, not many of Margaret's classmates came to see her off.

Among the few classmates who took leave from school was Cindy, who busily occupied Margaret in conversations and photo-taking. Margaret wasn't free for a single moment and did not even notice that Nathan and Tsz Ching were already standing in a corner away from the crowd, waiting patiently with no intention of interrupting her.

"Are they your friends?" asked her father, who was the first to notice them.

Following her father's hand movement, Margaret was happy that Nathan and Tsz Ching finally arrived. For some reason, Nathan looked a little shy and stood behind Tsz Ching, who was of course too small in size to shield him. Margaret ran over to hug both of them before introducing them to her father.

"I come to wish you all the best," said Tsz Ching and handed Margaret a small box. "For you. I bought these egg tarts for you, just in case you miss food from Hong Kong on the plane."

"Oh, thank you. That's very thoughtful of you," said Margaret. Turning to Nathan, she added, "Are you going to give me anything special?"

Nathan handed her a pop music magazine and said, "To help you kill time on the plane. I know it's a long flight."

"Two. We need to change planes in Vancouver." Margaret took the magazine from Nathan and was disappointed to see that it was in Chinese. "Sorry, I don't read Chinese magazines."

"You will read this one," said Nathan, giving Margaret a meaningful look.

Margaret didn't manage to find out Nathan's underlying meaning, for her aunt came over to suggest taking a group photo. After that, everybody wanted to spend a moment with her, being fully aware that the separation was going to last for years.

When her father announced it was time to leave, Margaret was still talking to her friends. Then came her father's warning: "We must go now, or we'll miss our flight," which prompted Nathan to go over to Margaret and hug her very tightly in his arms.

He whispered in her ear, "Read my card when you are alone." He held her for a good while before releasing her reluctantly.

Nobody had yet shed a single tear until Cindy started it. Already missing Margaret, she suddenly burst into tears. Anyone who witnessed her laughing fit would know that Cindy wasn't good at holding back her emotions. Tsz Ching quickly went over to comfort her, embracing her in her arms. She turned and said to Margaret, "You'd better go, or you'll miss your flight. I will take care of Cindy."

Before Margaret had time to thank Tsz Ching, she was pushed to the restricted area. Like Yang, she also turned round to take a good look at the crowd that came to see her off. Her eyes stayed longer on Nathan, who kept waving goodbye at her. He appeared to be in good control of his emotions, making sure that he didn't make a crying scene. Before Margaret stepped further inside, she could see Tsz Ching clinging onto Nathan's elbow. Rather than taking care of Cindy, she was now in charge of her boyfriend's well-being. Oddly enough, Margaret wasn't jealous on seeing this. They seemed to make a suitable pair—something of great harmony. She then tried to picture her own image next to Nathan's and was rather puzzled with what appeared in her mind's eye. It dawned on her, for the first time in her life, that her appearance was strikingly different from her peers.

Fortunately, there was no time to ponder who made a better match, for there were formalities to take care of at immigration and the customs. When completed, she finally managed to spend time on her own in a toilet. It's where she read Nathan's card that had been put inside the magazine. Margaret had no idea why he suddenly became so shy about his feelings and presented his card in disguise. The card was full of Nathan's declarations of love for Margaret, written in phrases borrowed from lyrics of pop songs. She wished he could be a bit more original, but of course she understood how demanding it was to write in a second language. When she considered her writing ability in Chinese, she felt ashamed. She was at least pleased that Nathan tried his best. His handwriting was neat and tidy. Other than the card, she also found a photo in the envelope. It was an image of a younger Nathan smiling and posing near a swimming pool. So, there she was, holding a card and a photo in her hands, running the events of that summer in her mind while trying to suppress her tears.

PART III
APRIL 2013
HONG KONG

A DINNER DATE

Fronted with professional graphics and a catchy one-liner printed in Helvetica, the proposal-turned-contract travelled safely in Margaret's Armani handbag that she also used as a briefcase. Competing in a men's world, she made a deliberate statement by refusing to use one of those standard leather bags. *I like my girlie stuff. I don't care what people think.* Certain things—in fact a lot of things—Margaret would compromise, but not what she wore or how she carried herself.

Margaret was on her way to the café at the Mandarin Hotel to meet an important client with whom she expected to close a deal, a contract that would recharge her bank account with a six-figure net. She was already making some mental plan of her next trip, probably in some villa in Bordeaux. Kate would most likely come with her unless she'd already made other plans. Both single, they usually spent Chinese New Year together on the top floor of Sheraton, gossiping about their friends over champagne and caviar. Not that they couldn't afford renting a room each, but it was more fun to sleep together in the penthouse suite. They would play all the silly pyjama games they invented over the years; they would do facial treatment and their nails together too.

A month had passed, and Margaret oscillated back to normal. She regained her momentum, and no longer reminisced her teenage years. Life went on as before. Most of the time she had her daily routine, occasionally a spa treatment and a shopping spree. She was resilient and wouldn't allow herself to be down for long, even though she was fully aware that Nathan had left her out of his life for a second time.

She still remembered how Nathan promised to come and visit her in Canada over and over again, and every time he let her down. Training had always been a convenient excuse. It made Margaret wonder if he cared enough to be bothered with being a little more creative. The same reason used over ten times? It wasn't even a lame excuse. It was dumb. Nathan was dumb to let Tsz Ching pick up the phone on that Christmas Eve when she called. Though furious, Margaret did not make a fuss. Besides, what could she do over a long-distance phone call? *Isn't Christmas a time to be with friends and family? And what's wrong with staying home, spending a quiet festival together?* she reasoned.

Her first year wasn't easy. It was particularly bad in the winter, punctuated with days that recorded punishingly low windchill factors. Along her way on the snowy paths to the bus stop, rushing to catch her six-thirty-in-the-morning bus, Margaret might not have much time for wild fantasies. But on her way home on days when it was less windy, she had a little free space in her mind to imagine Nathan standing at the corner of her street, waiting for her to come home, but of course her boyfriend from Hong Kong never materialised.

Their lifeline hinged upon the daily long-distance calls measured in hours. Margaret's mom would probably have left her alone if Nathan wasn't so tricky and made only collect calls. "Look at the bill. It's outrageous! You have to cut it down," Margaret's mom screamed the moment she opened the first phone bill. She would've had a heart attack had she known how cheap Nathan was, but Margaret didn't really mind about the expense. They were, after all, better off than Nathan's family, weren't they?

Margaret was definitely better off now that her client had put his signature down. After that, Margaret would be in charge of the whole project. First, she would secure a lease for a restaurant space in the Soho area. Then, she would spend time sourcing produce and ingredients of top quality. She would, of course, help recruit a team of local staff. So, when her client flew in with his team from Japan next time, they would be all set. As for now, she would take her Japanese client for a meal on the Peak. Window seats with a panoramic view were reserved, an '82 Lafite was ordered, and most important of all, the bill would be all paid for. Her client insisted. Why would Margaret argue against such generosity?

But the course of life could change very quickly in the age of technology. When Margaret's phone vibrated with a jazzy piano tune, she discreetly checked the text: "Let's meet tonight if you are free." It's also a one-liner, as catchy as, if not more so, than her own. To respond to this opportune life-changing event, Margaret had to think on her feet for a reasonable excuse to turn down her client.

Excuses made and accepted. *Sure, no problem, next time when I'm in town then. That's okay. I'm tired anyway.*

Margaret was perhaps still feeling a little guilty as she sent her client off in a taxi, but once she started her texting frenzy in the sparkling clean toilet of the Mandarin, her adrenaline shot up that made her skin glow and her hair shine. After a few rounds of texting back and forth, they agreed to meet on the Peak. And why not, since a table was already reserved? Nathan didn't have to know about her previous appointment.

Wow! They would finally meet again. *How many years now? Twenty? Well, let's see, it had to be more.*

Margaret couldn't wait and took a taxi all the way to the Peak. She had to make sure that there was time to powder her nose, in a manner of speaking, and present her best. Luckily, she had dressed properly for a date, a bit formal and not very sexy, but never mind, it would do for their first date after all these years.

Margaret had fun organising food and drinks with the manager, who knew her well. Keeping busy helped taking her mind off the upcoming meeting. Besides, she was just doing what she was good at. Making the dinner arrangements calmed her nerves, and now she had the time to wonder what made her so nervous. In her present state—divorced, experienced, and still irresistibly charming—she could start all over again with Nathan. But was that what she wanted? Was that what Nathan was after? Why did he finally agree to meet her after a month of silence?

An incoming text. *Oh, from Kate*: "How's it going?"

It took no time to send her back a reply: "Signed and sealed."

Almost immediately, Kate sent in her second one: "Congrats, have fun on the Peak."

Margaret knew they would do several rounds of texting until one of them couldn't spare any more time. In theory, she had the time. Nathan wouldn't arrive for another twenty minutes, perhaps more, but she wasn't in the mood to chat. Margaret spent slightly more time to compose her final message, in the hope of shutting her up: "Thanks. Something's come up. I'll call you later." It worked.

Two visits to the ladies room was more than enough to assure Margaret of her gorgeous look. A day's work seemed to have left no traces of fatigue on her face. The makeup, though not fresh, would still do. Her hair still looked bouncy from the morning wash, and lipstick reapplied to the right shape made her ruby-red lips look ever more attractive.

With nothing more to do, Margaret at last relaxed with a glass of red, watching the sky gradually losing its brightness. Nighttime came fast at this time of the year. It would be completely dark when Nathan arrived. *Better check my face in this lighting. Just one more time.*

Margaret was checking her mascara in a pocket-size mirror when she caught, from the corner of her eye, a pair of beige chino pants. *Oh, my God, he's finally here.* Margaret turned to him and only managed to exclaim, "Oh, I didn't expect . . . you!"

When they were sipping their second glass of Lafite after the first course, Margaret finally looked him in the eye and asked, "Why?"

"Why what?"

"Stop talking to me like that. You know full well what I'm saying."

"You must be disappointed."

"It's not that. I feel," Margaret bit her lip slightly before she said, "cheated."

"I'm really sorry. It was my idea."

"You mean he didn't even bother to reject me?" said Margaret. "That's unbelievable." As she was beginning to pour another glass, she asked, "So, it was you who wrote to me?"

"I did."

"Using his account?"

"That's right."

"But why?"

"When he told me that he wasn't going to do anything, I thought it was wrong. I think he owes you an explanation."

"About what?"

"Why he doesn't want to see you anymore, and why he doesn't want to talk about the past."

"So, why?" asked Margaret.

The arrival of the main course briefly interrupted their conversation, during which Margaret had a chance to look at her dinner companion, who was still in good shape and hadn't aged much.

As soon as the waitress walked away, Margaret couldn't help saying, "You look very fit."

"Oh, thank you. You are so kind." Alan added after a pause, "I wouldn't want to stand close to Nathan though. He's still athletic and hasn't aged a bit."

Margaret almost blurted out "I know," but managed to hold it and said instead, "But I won't ever see him again."

"I'm sorry."

"So, tell me, why doesn't he want to see me again?" asked Margaret.

"Well, because I think his life is such a mess, and he doesn't want you to know about it."

"Oh, that's something new," said Margaret with her eyebrows raised. "I always thought that he got everything he wanted. He's the champion, right?"

"Only in the pool, but not in life, not in relationships."

"I'm listening," said Margaret encouragingly.

"The thing is, soon after you left, they went steady."

"I know."

"You do?"

"Part of it, not the whole story though. Please go on," said Margaret, who somehow knew all about this already.

"The year you left, was it 1990 or '91, Nathan came in first in all the competitions."

"It was 1989, after the June fourth Tiananmen incident," corrected Margaret.

"Oh, yes. It might not be a good year for many people, but it was a wonderful year for Nathan. He hadn't lost, five years in a row, not even once. He was basically a hero in his school and all the swimming clubs. Nobody could resist him—his charm, his smile, and his good-looking body. I'll tell you what, I think I'd fall for him if I was a girl. And girls, they come and go so easily for Nathan, simply too easily and too fast."

"I thought he and Tsz Ching were a pair."

"Sure, but it didn't stop Nathan from fooling around. Every time after he broke up with his girl, he always went back to Tsz Ching, begging for forgiveness. And she always forgave him. I'm friends with both. What can I do?"

"Are they still together now?" asked Margaret.

"No, not that I know of. Anyway, I don't see much of Nathan. He spends a lot of time in China, which is why I sometimes help him check his social page. You know, he can't check it there. No access."

"Were they married?" asked Margaret.

"I don't know. Nobody knew for sure. We just heard rumours. Those were the years when we only met in the swimming club. We seldom talked, least of all about personal things. I think it was better that way. There are things that we'd better be discreet about."

"So how many years were they together?"

"Three or four, I don't remember. I don't know if they were legally married. Anyway, he was like blowing hot and cold about their relationship. If Tsz Ching hadn't been so tolerant, I don't think it would have lasted."

"Why?" sighed Margaret.

"Do you mean why Tsz Ching was so forgiving?"

"No, I mean why did Nathan treat her so badly," Margaret rephrased her question.

"Tsz Ching once asked me out for a drink. I suppose she was really depressed about their relationship and about life in general. She had no one to talk to anymore. I mean, how can you help somebody who repeats the same mistake over and over again? Her girlfriends must get tired of listening to her. Anyway, in her half-drunk, semi-conscious state of mind, she told me why."

Margaret posed a question mark on her face, although she didn't phrase it aloud.

"It's because of you. Nathan couldn't get over the fact that you dumped him. He's not used to being rejected."

"I didn't. He was always welcome to come and see me in Canada," Margaret said in a slightly-raised voice.

"I know, but don't forget how different the two of you are. Okay, maybe less so now. But you were from two different worlds then. Nathan wasn't even thinking of going to the university. He couldn't afford it. He was a nobody outside his swimming arena, and he was well aware of that."

"Oh, is that what was bothering him?" said Margaret.

"Personally, I think it's more than that. Nathan had always treated his romantic relationships rather lightly, until he met you. I think he just couldn't believe that he was head over heels in love. He was scared, if you ask me."

"Is that the reason why he treated Tsz Ching so badly?" asked Margaret.

"I know it doesn't make sense. In a way, Tsz Ching asked for it. She kept reminding him of you, about your good looks and about how happy you made him. She was, of course, so jealous of you that she couldn't think straight. What a wrong strategy! Every time they had a fight, they always came back to the same issue. They always fought about the past, his past with you. I got fed up with him yelling at her and then her screaming and crying about taking her life. In the end, I just had to stop seeing them both."

"It must be really bad for Tsz Ching to want to kill herself," said Margaret in a sympathetic voice.

"They were threats only. People don't usually kill themselves if they talk so much about it. Only those quiet ones actually do it, like our friend."

"What do you mean?"

"Haven't you heard? It's our friend, Dominic. He killed himself."

"No, you must be joking. Why?" Margaret couldn't believe what she heard.

"How do I know? He never talked to anyone. He kept himself to himself. All I know was that he killed himself after he came back from his trip to America. Or was it Canada?"

"When was it?"

"Must've been a month or two before the handover, sometime in May or June. I don't remember. You know, that was the time when everyone was eagerly waiting for the big day, wondering how the handover would affect us. I read it in the paper, somewhere in the briefs. It was so long ago that I can't recall what I read. What I don't understand is, how could he kill himself by drowning? I mean as a swimmer myself, it's just incredible. Margaret, are you all right?"

Her dinner companion stopped his narration when he saw her looking away, wiping tears streaming down her cheeks with a cloth napkin.

"Why are you so upset?" asked Alan. "We didn't really know much of Dominic. He was just a friend."

"You don't understand. Dominic was more than a friend," said Margaret after she calmed down a little.

"Let's not spoil our dinner. All I remember is how blunt and how different he was from any of us."

That was exactly why Margaret felt so upset about the news. Dominic was indeed different from any of her teenage friends. He probably was the only one who truly accepted Margaret as a local. He never set boundaries of what Margaret should or should not do. Nor did he ever challenge her identity as a Hong Kong girl. How she missed such a friend!

PART IV
MARCH 1997
WINNIPEG

A COLD WAR

Sitting in front of the fireplace with the wind howling outside, Margaret couldn't help feeling a sense of self-pity even though there was a full supply of Kahlua with milk. Mom was sure to stock up on food and essentials before she left. The shelves in the pantry were so stuffed with food and drink that Margaret couldn't get anything out without knocking down some on the floor. But what's the fun of drinking and eating by herself?

Mom, why is there so much food? Who is it for? I thought you would only go for a month.

Even if the food was meant for her and Brent, Margaret wasn't convinced. Besides, her mother knew that they were supposed to have a split-up—yes, again, for the fourth time since they were together.

Margaret sighed, picked up her drink from the side table, put it down without touching it, and then sighed again before her mom's new pup started licking her feet.

"Stop it." Margaret always had issues with soft touch and couldn't help giggling. She tried to push the little dog away but didn't manage to stop her canine friend from showing her friendliness. The more she pushed, the more the dog wanted to get near her. When the little pup finally calmed down, she looked at Margaret, without blinking her beady eyes.

"Now what?" Not understanding the meaning of Margaret's words, her little companion had her head tilted. "So, you are hungry again?" That's the cue she knew. On hearing it, the little dog ran towards the kitchen, leading a few paces ahead.

Together they ran to the well-stocked kitchen where there was enough for a family for a month or two. Margaret had a secret feeling that her mother made all these preparations so that she wouldn't have any excuse for leaving home and that her pet would be well looked after.

Speedily, the dog wolfed down her food, literally in seconds, just long enough for Margaret to make her routine speech in Cantonese. "Snowy is such a silly name, I'll call you Bei-bei. I'll make you a clever, bilingual dog."

There was no reason to name her mother's dog in Cantonese other than to annoy her. Since the first day, Margaret had been teaching the new pup a few tricks, such as shaking hands and playing dead. Instead of giving commands in English, she always used Cantonese. When the dog first learned to put her paw on Margaret's hand, she called her "Bei-bei," which literally meant "Give, give."

Betty gritted her teeth and complained, but Margaret always challenged her, "Why can't I teach her Cantonese? Bei-bei will be bilingual, like me." Subconsciously, she was trying to keep the language, which was gradually losing its significance in her life. Here in Canada, she happily immersed in Western culture, feeling completely at ease with her new identity. She cleverly adjusted her accent to even speak like a Canadian. Since she spoke to no one in Cantonese, the new dog came in useful as a silent language partner.

At a time when her mother was trying to bond with her new pup, she wouldn't have agreed to make a trip back to Hong Kong had her husband's business not been in crisis. Her mom always had a way with people she knew at Hong Kong's Canadian Chamber of Commerce. She would pull a few strings, and everything would be fine.

So that was the plan: her parents would be away for a month or so. By the time they returned, winter would be over. The weather would then be warm enough for them to go out and see friends. When the wind wasn't so severe, they would be able to take the dog out for walks. Of course, when they left, they did not expect Winnipeg was going to be hit by the flood of the century, which would change many people's lives.

As Margaret was about to walk back to the sitting area, she felt a tug at the edges of her pants. "What's up?" Bei-bei gave a few barks. "Now? Okay, be a good girl. Just hold it, okay?"

Together they ran downstairs to the basement where her father kept his expensive red wine, a freezer, a washing machine, and a dryer. Unlike some of their neighbours who turned their basement into a second living room, theirs was unfurnished. Nothing was more suitable than an uncarpeted basement for house-training new puppies.

It didn't take long for Bei-bei to finish her business. Very soon, they were back in the warm, cozy sitting area where Margaret had left her drink untouched. "Now, I can at last enjoy myself."

Margaret looked at the clock on the wall. Nine o'clock. For someone who never went to bed before midnight, there were still a few hours to kill. For some reason, Margaret felt edgy and wasn't in the mood to indulge herself in this solo drinking act. Now that the puppy was fast asleep in a basket next to her, a sense of self-pity suddenly arose. Staring at the second hand on the wall, her eyes were glued to its movement. The constant, regular tick-tock motion had a calming effect. Watching the clock tick and counting the number of seconds in her head, she asked herself if anything had changed in the last minute. Had she become older and wiser? Did the minute that had just passed have any effect on her life? Margaret did not want to ponder over the past nor think about the future; she might as well be focusing on her present state of mind.

Since she had no plans to call Brent, she had to make sure that she had every comfort at hand to stop feeling sorry for herself.

Playing some music was absolutely necessary. She put on her favourite CD of Alanis Morissette and sang along to "Head over Feet" over and over again until she decided it was time to get some crisps from the pantry. Now, she felt content, sipping her drink, snacking and listening to her favourite music, like a princess, even without Brent by her side. The good thing about being his girlfriend was that she was treated as if she were the most precious and the dearest. Brent always bought her expensive presents and took her to high-class restaurants that she hadn't known of before they met.

They knew each other by chance, one that really had the lowest probability. On a day when Margaret covered for her classmate Carol, who was too sick to work her lunch shift, Brent came in for a meal. He wouldn't normally choose this restaurant along Pembina Highway, but he had no choice when his client's secretary told him that her boss was stuck in a previous appointment downtown. It would be better for Brent to have lunch first.

To avoid disappointment, Brent made a safe choice: a beefsteak burger and a glass of coke. He ordered his food while he was busy reading the document without making any eye contact with the waitress. He wasn't even listening to a cheerful voice that presented the specials of the day and the chef's recommendations.

"Are you sure you don't want to try our scallops? They are very fresh, just arrived this morning," said Margaret with slight irritation in her voice. She didn't like customers rushing through their order without listening to her presentation. Her feelings were hurt, albeit slightly.

"Now you are tempting me." Brent put down the file and moved his eyes to the waitress standing in front of him. Almost immediately, he became speechless, for he had never seen someone so attractive before. Brent did not know any Eurasians, and he only socialised with people from his own background, so he found Margaret's type rather unusual. What he didn't know at the time was that this woman's beautiful features were a combination of Western and Eastern blood. He was intrigued by a certain subtlety in her beauty, something rather unusual in women of her age. Would a goddess from stories of classical mythology look like her?

"I would highly recommend it," said Margaret. "Today's not very busy. The chef will give his best to the house special."

"I will definitely go for it." As Brent was passing the menu back to Margaret, he asked for the wine menu.

"I thought you wanted a soft drink," said Margaret.

"A burger to go with a soft drink, no problem. But now, with a gourmet lunch, how can I not order a glass of wine?"

So, a glass of wine turned into two, then three, until Brent asked Margaret to leave the whole bottle of Muscat Blanc on the table. It was a mistake to assume that Brent did this to impress Margaret. The fact was that his client's secretary came in to deliver a second message, informing him that it would at least be another hour before her boss could attend the meeting. An apology was made and accepted in the most civil manner. The secretary was surprised that Brent took this inconvenience so lightly.

How could Brent not be in a fine mood? From where he was sitting, he had a full view of his goddess walking gracefully between a few tables, serving food and drinks as though her work was effortless.

When Margaret finished serving all her customers, she came over to check and see whether Brent needed anything else.

"No, I am fine. My client should be here any minute."

"All right, just let me know if I can be of any help before I'm off," said Margaret.

"Oh, it's so late. I'd better settle my bill. I don't want to keep you."

"It's no problem at all." Margaret showed her understanding with a smile. "It must be boring to be waiting and reading the document over and over again." Realising what she had said was too personal, she quickly added, "Oh, it's really none of my business. Please don't mind what I said."

"That's fine. You are absolutely right about the document. I have read it so many times that I've learned it by heart," said Brent. "The strange thing about this client of mine is that he's usually very punctual. For him to be so late, I am a little worried."

It was as though his client wanted to reassure Brent of his well-being; he arrived at the most opportune moment. His client, Eric, felt so apologetic that he not only signed the contract after Brent briefly explained it, but he also settled the lunch bill. Margaret only had to serve them coffee before she left. It had been the most wonderful and fruitful afternoon for Brent, who first had a full lunch with good seafood and tasty wine, and further managed to close a deal with profitable terms for his company. How could he not thank his beautiful goddess for bringing him such luck?

"You must forgive me for being so late," said Eric over his last sip of coffee. "It won't happen again. If you'll excuse me, I must see my secretary before she calls it a day."

"Of course," said Brent absentmindedly. "I need to make those amendments in our contract too. Thank you very much for lunch. It was so generous of you."

"By the way, how was it?"

"Fantastic, I highly recommend it," said Brent with great enthusiasm.

"We must eat together next time," said Eric.

"How about next Thursday? My treat." Brent thought it would be more likely to see Margaret again if he came back on the same weekday.

"Maybe, I'll check with my secretary and get back to you later. She knows my schedule better than I do," said Eric before he dashed off.

How could Brent bear to wait another week? Before his lunch appointment with Eric, he ate by himself two more times—dinner on Saturday and then lunch on the following Monday. Although he sat at the same table, he saw no sign of his goddess. Business was good, even on a Monday, so Brent had to order a full course with wine to secure his table without feeling guilty.

When he finally paid his bill, he couldn't help asking the waitress who served him for the second time, "I think I left my pen on this table when I ate here last week. Could you please check and see if the waitress kept it for me?" Brent thought it a good reason to ask about his goddess this way.

"Which waitress? I'm afraid nobody mentioned anything to me. Let me check with the hostess. When did you lose your pen? Do you remember?"

"It was Thursday last week, I think," said Brent.

"Oh, I was sick on that day. Which table were you at?" asked Carol.

"Here, at the same table," said Brent.

"Oh, it would have been Margaret. She doesn't work here. She was only here to cover for me on my sick leave. Anyway, I can still check with the hostess for you. She may know something about your pen." Brent started feeling sorry for lying to the young lady who was extremely helpful and trustful.

When Carol walked back to his table with a negative answer, Brent said to her, "I might have made a mistake. I could have left my pen anywhere. I am sorry to cause you the trouble."

"No problem. I'll keep looking out for the pen for you," said Carol. "What is it like?"

Brent made up a short description of his missing pen that did not exist. Seeing that the waitress was walking away, he grabbed his last chance and added, "But surely your friend is so professional, it can't be her first time waiting on tables."

"Oh no, she is more experienced than any of us here. She's been working in different restaurants too. I don't think I could work in a Japanese restaurant like she does, all the cooking and preparations she makes in front of her customers. That requires way too much concentration; also, the customers are closely watching you. I don't think I could handle it."

"She must be good at it." Brent tried to encourage Carol to say more.

"Oh yes, she is, and that's how she gets good tips."

"You don't mean the restaurant near the Bay Department Store, do you?"

"Yes, that's the one. There aren't too many restaurants that require waitresses to cook and serve at the table. It's quite a package: good atmosphere, good service, and reasonable food. I suppose that's what people like."

"I've passed that restaurant many times, but it never occurred to me to give it a try. I don't know why."

"Maybe you don't like Japanese food?"

"How do I know if I haven't tried it before?" responded Brent in a meaningful way.

Whether he liked Japanese food or not was not a matter of importance. Before he knew it, he was already eating there by himself. It wasn't difficult to strike up a conversation with Margaret, since she remembered him very well. How could she not? If it had not been for him, she would have finished duty much earlier, but she gave him such a good-natured smile that you wouldn't think she minded it at all.

Things happened so quickly that it took a while to recall what the sequence of events was. Did Brent eat at the Japanese restaurant for a second time before they had their first date? Did they go and watch a movie or eat in a restaurant the first time they went out? Margaret had almost no recollection of these details. If they watched a movie, it probably was one with a confusing plot, unattractive characters, and lines finishing at midsentence.

When Margaret tried to remember when they had sex for the first time, it was even harder. Was it before or after she bought her first car? It wasn't because the matter was unimportant to her. The fact was her mind was occupied with the final paper she was supposed to submit for graduation during that time. Having already deferred for a term, she could not afford delaying it a second time. Besides, her not remembering was mainly due to all the girl talk on the topic of sex. Margaret had heard so much about her friends' love stories and sex lives that she even started talking about hers in such a convincing way that nobody would guess that she was still a virgin. It was like someone repeatedly listening to others' travel experiences and then fantasizing their own visit to a tourist spot. When they finally had a chance to visit the place, they would most likely say, "Been there. Seen it!"

For some reason she felt embarrassed for her inexperience, for being a virgin—that is, technically speaking, if her intimate encounters with Nathan didn't count. Though she was blurred with the date, Margaret clearly remembered how she tried to act normal and natural in the hope that Brent wouldn't find out that he was her first man. But how could she hide the discomfort and pain of first sex? So, when Brent checked with her afterwards, she had to admit it by making a soft reply, "Uh-huh," at his back.

What Margaret didn't expect was that her timid appearance only encouraged more passion.

Sex after the first time was much easier and more enjoyable. Margaret now began to better understand her own body, and of course that of Brent's. In the beginning, she was happy to be guided all the way through, but as her experience grew, she became much bolder with her movements. Making good use of her flexibility, she gained a lot of pleasure from her act and was sure that Brent enjoyed it too. There was, however, one thing missing from their lovemaking experience; there was no music in her ears. Neither did she see patterns of colours in her mind's eye, something that she rather missed but was not sure she would ever experience again. She wondered if she had really experienced that blissful moment before or if she had only imagined it.

This all happened last year. Their relationship had now developed into a steady stage that in fact wasn't completely steady. Overall, Margaret found Brent a very good boyfriend, more than good actually, especially when she compared him with her girlfriends'. But to Margaret, buying her expensive presents and taking her places wasn't good enough. She needed more. For one thing, she wanted him to be honest with her. Not that Brent was being unfaithful, she just wanted him to be truthful about everything. With no real work experience other than waiting on tables, Margaret hadn't thought how difficult it was for a top salesman to always tell the complete truth. It was hard to imagine why Brent always kept something from her, even though it didn't bring any major consequence. Wouldn't it be easier to tell her everything rather than covering a lie with another one, particularly when he was dealing with someone he loved?

Equally challenging for Brent to understand was why his girlfriend made so much fuss over a white lie. Margaret's background was completely different from his; that much he knew. Perhaps the main difference lay in their upbringing, or to be precise, their mothers. Her mother wasn't exactly manipulative, but Betty was strict with Margaret. Since she was little, she had to follow rules and orders so much that being honest was naturally her top priority.

Their different backgrounds meant that they usually had a lot to say to one another, especially when they were in good moods, but occasionally conflicts arose, and they could possibly lead to break-ups. In the last three times after a big row, Brent did everything to make it up to her. He had to have spent a month's salary on flowers and chocolate. And why shouldn't he? Wasn't a romantic relationship supposed to be like this?

A VISITOR

Margaret expected a similar pattern of resolving this new conflict, except that she wouldn't make it so easy for Brent this time. Having decided to teach him a lesson, she refused to answer any of his phone calls. She also changed her daily routine so completely that Brent wouldn't know when she would be home. She was only a little concerned about her friends' integrity. Not that her girlfriends would betray her, but they might be bribed, or one of them might start feeling sorry for Brent and tip him off. To avoid this, Margaret had stopped seeing her girlfriends too.

With the new pup, Margaret managed rather well being on her own without feeling lonely, until tonight. Perhaps the cold war had lasted for too long. Not even her favourite drink and music brought much comfort. The sound of the wind made her feel rather empty.

She must have been staring at the phone for so long that when it finally rang it gave her a fright. Having restored her calmness, she curved her mouth up into a big, satisfied smile. No matter how much she wanted to answer it, she had to keep her cool. She must not act too eager; better still, her voice had to show some irritation—not a lot, but just enough to raise concern for the caller—over a phone call late at night.

Margaret let the phone ring for a while before picking it up. She counted to make sure that Brent would not think that she wasn't home. On its seventh ring, Margaret breathed in a "Hello" over the receiver. Anyone who heard her greeting would have thought that Margaret had just rushed in to pick up the call.

On receiving no reply, she said "Hello" again. This time, she heard someone say "Hello" in Cantonese. Strange. Who was calling her? Nobody spoke to her in Cantonese other than her father and Aunt Jennifer.

"Who do you want?" asked Margaret in Cantonese.

"Is Margaret there?"

"Speaking. Who are you?"

"Oh, is that really you? This is Dominic."

Expecting a different phone call, Margaret was lost for words.

"Can you hear me?" asked Dominic. "Do you remember me?"

"Oh, yes. Dominic, friend from Hong Kong, right? Are you calling from Hong Kong? We haven't met for so long."

"No, I am now in Canada—Winnipeg, actually. Can you come and pick me up?"

"Pick you up?" repeated Margaret in disbelief. "From where?"

"At the Greyhound bus terminus."

"Have you booked accommodations?" asked Margaret. "Where are you staying?"

"I'm staying at your place, I hope. That's what I called you for," said Dominic. "Can you come now? I don't have much change left."

What was Dominic thinking? His request was most unreasonable and absurd. How did he expect someone whom he had not met for years to react? But on a cold, windy night, Margaret didn't have the heart to turn an old friend away, no matter how brief their encounter was. After all, Dominic did remind her of a period in her life that still gave her pangs of jealousy and bitter feelings.

When Margaret sat on the same sofa an hour later, she was no longer alone. She had made two car trips to and from the bus terminus. And now Dominic was eating a bowl of noodles she cooked for him. She finally had the chance of observing his face as he was slowly munching his food. In front of her was no longer a boyish face. There were a few lines, no matter how faint, around his large, hollow eyes. Unlike years ago, he was now muscular and much taller than before. He had shed that sickly complexion that used to cause scorn and ridicule among friends. An illumination from the fireplace made his face appear bigger than what it actually was, which was why his sunken cheeks were quite out of place. Margaret reasoned that it had to be the long bus journey that gave him a look of fatigue.

When Dominic finally finished eating, he returned his gaze to Margaret. "What are you looking at?"

"I'm sorry," said Margaret. "I just wonder how much you have changed."

"How have I changed?"

"Your face seems to be different than before. If you had not called me first, I wouldn't have recognised you. Even your voice has changed."

It was true that now Dominic spoke in a deep, manly voice, not much different to that of a baritone.

"I'm the same. I've just grown older."

"That's not true," protested Margaret. "You've only become stronger and more mature. I mean, we are both older. I am older now."

"It's not the same. I feel old," said Dominic.

Finding the topic a little awkward, Margaret changed the subject. "So, are you here on holiday? How long are you going to be here for?"

"I made a request of transferring some money here. As soon as I get it, I'll buy a plane ticket and leave. Can I stay in your place while I am waiting? It won't take long."

"I didn't mean that. But surely you must have bought your return ticket if you've come for a holiday? Everyone does."

"No, I didn't. I thought I would stay in Canada for good."

"So, have you changed your mind?"

Instead of answering her question, Dominic asked, "Can I have some more noodles, please?"

"Oh, sure."

Despite the changes in his appearance, Dominic's way of communication was the same as before—short, blunt, and incoherent—but rather than being angry at him, Margaret felt completely at home. Dominic was so predictable that she even felt a little nostalgic about her younger days. This unexpected visit of his reminded her of the stay that he and his friend made at her place in Hong Kong.

"What happened to your friend? You know, the one I had to play his girlfriend?" asked Margaret.

"I don't want to talk about him."

They dropped the subject and did not touch upon it anymore that night. They talked about something else. Since Dominic did not keep in touch with any of their friends in common, they mainly talked about things in general, for example, the changes in Hong Kong over the last few years. When Margaret finished her drink and did all the washing-up, it was already one in the morning.

Dominic slept for twelve hours after a second bowl of noodles. Margaret, for a change, did not sleep well. She was very much disturbed by the wind and the fact that she was not alone in the house. Even Bei-bei was more alert than usual; she would prick up her ears at the slightest sound and start barking. All these things did not make it easy for Margaret to fall asleep. When she finally did, she had all those weird dreams, one of which was so real that she wondered if she actually did walk for hours in an unknown city trying to look for a toilet in response to a call of nature. When she finally managed to find a public toilet near a park, she was disappointed and shocked to find that there was no toilet bowl inside any of the cubicles. In each of them was a low table covered with an orange cloth. A few candles were placed on the tabletop, burning, giving out an orange halo on the walls. Waking up from her dream, Margaret couldn't help remembering that somebody she knew did use a female public toilet as a place of refuge. She wondered what happened to Yang after he left Hong Kong.

Dominic was a very easy-going visitor. He did not request to see places and made no fuss over food. Unlike some of her father's friends who would start missing barbeque pork, dim sum, and fried noodles right from day one, Dominic was happy with any food, as long as she cooked him a bowl of noodles for his midnight supper. At first, Margaret thought that this unusual eating pattern was due to jet lag. Later, she found out that

Dominic had started this eating habit a few years ago when he took up his night shift working as a hotel receptionist.

Margaret did find out more about Dominic's life in his short visit. Not that Dominic was much of a conversationalist, but Margaret was patient and asked her questions at the right time. It wasn't long before she got to know him quite well. The weather was still pretty chilly in Winnipeg. Though this year wasn't as cold as it should have been, they didn't want to stay outdoors for more than five minutes. To avoid feeling miserably cold and numb, they spent most of their time in shopping malls and restaurants, where they talked a lot. They did not make long conversations like most old friends did, so, to make a coherent account, Margaret had to piece together his short and usually unfinished comments.

There was one afternoon they went browsing in a nearby shopping mall for the purpose of killing time before dinner. As they were walking past an ice-cream shop, Margaret said casually, "Would you like an ice-cream?"

"No, and you?" said Dominic.

"No, not really," said Margaret. "I was only checking to see if you like ice-cream like most of my friends. One of them, in particular, has what you call a sweet tooth. Every time she sees an ice-cream shop, she can't resist the temptation, even though she is supposed to be on a diet. But the thing is, she never succeeds. She could be on a strict diet for days until she walks into an ice-cream shop. She would then come out feeling so guilty and so bad about herself that she would start her diet all over again. I really feel sorry for her."

"Do you? I don't. I don't feel sorry for anyone who has too much to eat. I don't feel sorry for people who have too much of everything. If you hold three jobs like me, the concern about food is when one has the time to eat and what he should eat to last till the next meal."

"Three jobs? Wow! How did you do that? I found it hard to work part-time in my university years. I'm glad it's now over."

"I'm glad for you too, but I don't see an end to this life for me."

"Why not? Haven't you planned to move here? You can stay in Canada and find a job. I can help you find one. I can't guarantee life is a lot better here, but I don't think you need to do three jobs to earn a living. It's much easier to get by. Who knows, you may go to university one day," said Margaret encouragingly.

"I told you already. I changed my plans. As soon as my brother sends me the money, I'll buy my plane ticket and leave."

They kept strolling in the mall until they came to the front of a shop that specialised in sportswear. Margaret couldn't help thinking of Nathan. What happened was that, although the two young lovers talked a lot over the phone in the first year of Margaret's arrival in Canada, they never saw one another again. As the years went by, the number of phone calls gradually decreased until the two of them stopped pretending they cared anymore. In the first year when the flame was still burning, they talked excitedly about Nathan's visit to Winnipeg, and each time when the date neared, something seemed to come up that forced him to cancel his trip. There were at least two such occasions that made Margaret feel utterly disappointed, not so much at the change of plans, but more at Nathan's unwillingness to uphold the decision. However, on the other hand, Margaret understood that as a rising star in the swimming arena, Nathan had to follow a very rigid training schedule.

"I know you don't see much of our old friends," said Margaret as she was looking at a collection of swimwear on a rack. "But if you do, I'm sure you'll feel proud of Nathan."

"Why?" asked Dominic.

"He's now the champion swimmer of Hong Kong. Don't you know? I bet Tsz Ching must be very proud of him." After a moment of silence, Margaret said again, "Are you still seeing Tsz Ching? You used to go to the same school, isn't that right?"

"Yes, we did, but that was a long time ago. I haven't seen her since we finished secondary school. I don't know what happened to her."

"Do you see any of your old classmates? Don't you have any reunions?"

"Maybe my classmates do, but I never contact any of them. I spend pretty much all my waking hours working. I'm hardly home. Even if my friends call, they won't be able to get hold of me."

"Come on, it's you and your three jobs again. But how come you managed to write to me all these years?"

"Writing to you is different. I can write during my night shifts; it's usually not very busy. Besides, I can practise my English."

That was how much Dominic was willing to say at one time. Margaret would have to wait for the next time when he was in the mood to talk again. In later conversations, Margaret came to know more about Dominic's three jobs. During the day, he worked as a warehouse manager, which meant he had to do everything, including checking stock, arranging deliveries, and moving goods around himself. No wonder he was so much more muscular than before. He was efficient at work and usually finished around four o'clock. To earn a little extra money before his night shift, he also worked as a private tutor. Three times a week he would go to a family and coach their six-year-old son in simple mathematics and English. His student was smart and did not require too much attention. Only during exam period was he required to work overtime. His job at the hotel, according to Dominic, was the least demanding. He had basically nothing much to do after midnight. As long as he stayed alert and was able to pick up calls within a few seconds, he could do anything he liked. His night activities were first eating a bowl of noodles, then writing letters or reading before napping for a few hours. He would always wake up at five, giving himself an hour to freshen up before his colleague took over the morning shift. All he needed was two hours to get home for a shower before starting another day.

Margaret had no idea how he managed such a life and what motivated him to do so. She was discreet and didn't ask him any direct questions, particularly on matters about money. There was one time when Dominic volunteered to disclose his financial status by telling Margaret that it took him four years to save up enough for this trip. Although it didn't seem right, she dared not challenge him. Anyone with a sound mind could work out that a trip to Canada, no matter how luxurious it was, did not cost that much. So, Dominic had to save up for something else other than *just* a trip to Canada. He once talked about settling down here, so perhaps the money was for a new life?

During the time when Dominic was enjoying Margaret's hospitality, she had, in a way, made up with Brent over the phone, but she made it clear that she would see him only after her visitor was gone. What torture the separation was for Brent, Margaret didn't care. She was eager to find out more about her old friend who was unquestionably shrouded in an air of mystery. Margaret found that most intriguing.

As the days passed, Dominic's patience waiting for his brother's remittance was wearing thin.

"Do you mind if I make a phone call to Hong Kong? I must speak to my brother about the money."

"Sure, you can use the phone in the kitchen," said Margaret. "Take your time. I'll take a shower before we go out for some shopping and lunch."

Subconsciously, Margaret thought it good manners to leave Dominic alone so he could discuss financial and possibly domestic matters with his brother in private. To give him more time, she also painted her nails and did a facial treatment at a leisurely pace in her parents' bathroom. Most of what Dominic said over the phone went unheard, even though the bathroom was not far from the kitchen and the walls were not soundproof. He deliberately lowered his voice to a whisper, so Margaret couldn't make out what he said, although she could vaguely hear his voice.

Waiting for the nail polish to dry, she had nothing better to do but check her eyebrows in the mirror. Margaret wasn't exactly a narcissist, but with an image that showed the right skin tone and the features to their right size and proportion, she couldn't help being pleased at her own reflection. It was picture perfect.

In the midst of her self-indulgence, she was suddenly alarmed by Dominic, who started cursing and swearing in his raised voice. Margaret didn't realise that Dominic had such a powerful voice, and she nearly thought that he had stormed into the bathroom. Involuntarily, she covered herself with a towel, tiptoed to the door, and put her ear close to the door slit. She could now hear pretty much every single word coming from the kitchen. She considered herself a concerned friend and wasn't at all ashamed of listening behind the door. When the phone call was over, she gathered that Dominic went broke. There was no money left in his bank account, and his brother refused to lend him any. This was quite different from what Dominic had been expecting all along.

Margaret wasn't quite sure what she was supposed to say to him over lunch. Had she better act normal, as if she didn't know anything about it? Or should she offer her help? She could easily lend him the money if Dominic's pride did not get in the way. As she was considering her options, she heard that Dominic was making a second phone call. *My poor friend must be calling his brother again!* she thought.

It didn't take long before Margaret realised that she was wrong. Although she wasn't sure who Dominic was calling this time, it was clearly not his brother. Dominic didn't say much in the second phone call, but between long silences occasionally filled with sighs and simple responses, Margaret could clearly hear him speak in Mandarin. Within seconds, Margaret guessed that it had to be Yang. She couldn't explain her impulsive idea, but once the name crossed her mind, she was quite settled on that. Perhaps it was Dominic's reaction to her question about Yang the other day that made her connect his call with this person. While he wasn't bothered with any of his friends in Hong Kong, Dominic clearly showed a special interest in Yang. Where would he be now?

When Margaret was done with her beauty ritual, it had to be half an hour later. She reasoned that Dominic had to have finished his phone calls by now. Walking into the kitchen in her simple T-shirt and jeans, she made an effort of making herself sound cheerful. "I'm ready, are you?"

Dominic was sitting in a corner, hardly moving at all. Running towards her was Bei-bei, who must have been sleeping beside him, keeping him company all the while. Now, standing on the spot that had been warmed by Bei-bei's body heat, she felt a sudden pang of sympathy for her friend. Margaret felt sorry for her friend's extreme melancholy that was completely beyond her understanding.

***

To cheer him up after his difficult phone calls, Margaret suggested staying home to cook Dominic a nice dinner. Over a relaxed meal, he would perhaps open up about his troubles. Margaret would then get to know him better; she would also get news about Hong Kong through his stories. Since she had moved to Canada, she gradually lost contact with her old friends. In spite of her efforts, she began to lose interest in their way of life.

When she was still in her high-school years, Margaret was so excited about spending her summer vacations in Hong Kong. She longed to see her friends, but each time it turned out to be a great disappointment. The jokes they used to share and laugh at were no longer funny. Her sentiment for Hong Kong was mainly driven by her wish to see Nathan again. So, when he excluded her from his life, she felt a sense of betrayal and suddenly lost interest in the place and its people. The things that Cindy cared about suddenly seemed so trivial to Margaret that she had difficulty paying attention when they talked. It was as though her friends felt the same. Their summer reunions were getting more and more infrequent. The ones that took place were not well-attended. People came up with all sorts of reasons for not coming. In the last one, even Cindy did not bother to show up.

Dominic was now her last friend from Hong Kong. After all, he was the only one who cared to write to her. Talking to

Dominic made her feel nostalgic. Oh, how she wished to be learning Japanese with her friends again! Wouldn't it be nice if she could just dream about the future without the baggage of the past? Was it possible to feel old at the age of twenty-two?

Working in restaurants for years had improved almost nothing but her standards for the taste of food. Margaret could now categorise any cuisine into different grades, from fine and exquisite to something that was barely edible. Her knowledge had also pushed her cooking skills to a higher level. She chose the best ingredients for even a simple meal. The time and effort she put into preparing, cooking, and presenting a dish always paid off. She knew from her experience working as a waitress that it wasn't just the taste of food, but also its presentation that enriched one's dining experience. And that was what Margaret hoped to create for Dominic tonight.

After the appetizer and a glass of wine, Dominic started to loosen up. Deliberately, Margaret arranged their dinner at an extremely slow pace. So, when they started eating their main course, Dominic was well into his second glass.

Margaret was quite sure of Dominic's willingness to talk when he said, "I enjoy your cooking. Really, I do. I've never had such nice food before. You would never imagine what life was like for me in the past few years."

"I'm glad you like my cooking. I'm afraid we Canadians don't do much except eat and drink, mostly in people's homes and sometimes in restaurants."

"Can I ask you something?"

"Sure."

"Are you truly a Canadian?"

"Of course. Why do you ask?"

"Even though you were not born here?"

"Why not? It's not important." There was then a silence, during which Margaret considered Dominic's question that she had never thought of before. "Do you think I cannot be a Canadian if I wasn't born here? If not, what am I?"

"Do you not consider yourself Chinese?"

"I'm half Chinese."

"I don't mean that. Don't you feel that you belong to Hong Kong?"

"No, not really. Wait, sometimes . . . only when I go back to Hong Kong for my holidays. Even so, I can't say I belong to a place."

"Do you mean you don't feel being connected to Hong Kong anymore?"

Margaret thought for a moment and said, "No, I'm afraid not."

"I see. You are both the same."

"Who are you talking about?"

"You and my friend Yang. You both want to forget about your past."

"Excuse me. I don't know who and what you're talking about."

"You want to forget about Nathan, and Yang wants to forget about his country."

"Did I hear that right? You think I want to forget about Nathan? That's something new. I'll tell you what. I've already forgotten about him."

"That's what Yang thinks too."

"I don't know about your friend Yang and his country, but I certainly think no more of Nathan."

Margaret now got so excited about this conversation that she poured another glass, first for herself, then another one for Dominic, who disagreed with her. "I don't think you have forgotten about him. I don't think you ever will."

"Why not?"

"Because both of you will never forget that you were betrayed."

"By his country?"

"No, you got muddled with your Cantonese. I mean you feel betrayed by Nathan because he didn't keep his promise. He didn't live up to your expectations. You expected him to come and visit you, but he never did. What's more, every time you go back to Hong Kong, he found some excuse to avoid seeing you."

"Really? So you understand my feelings better than I do. What about Yang?"

"Oh, he's even worse. He's now completely changed himself into a Canadian. He refuses to talk about the past. He acts as if he has nothing to do with China anymore."

"So Yang is now in Canada?"

"Yes, of course. Why do you think I planned to move to Canada?"

Margaret found his reply absurd, but she didn't want to contradict Dominic, or he might change his mind and stop talking altogether. Instead, she asked, "I sometimes think of him too. So, how is Yang? What is he doing in Canada?"

"Oh, he's doing very well now. He started teaching in the university last year, in small classes. He's now studying for his doctorate."

"Wow, he must be very clever. How long has he lived in Canada?" Margaret was thinking of her last meeting with Yang.

"He's clever enough, but mind you, he was already studying in his final year in China. He spent the first few years catching up with his English. When he first arrived in America, he could read and write quite well, by the Chinese standard anyway, but his spoken English was almost nonexistent."

"So he went to America first? For him to be able to teach in the university now, he must have worked very hard."

"Not much harder than I had to. Of course, I thought we both did it for our future."

"How do you mean?"

Rather than giving his reply, Dominic acted in his usual way of posing a question. "Why do you think I needed three jobs?"

Being completely lost, Margaret asked, "So, why?"

Dominic took a deep breath before he said this in one stretch, "Because I needed the money to support him. I'd been sending him money all these years so he could finish his undergraduate and postgraduate studies without worrying about his finance. Who knows, he might even have some money left to send home. You see, he still has to support his parents in China. I usually gave him enough to last for two months, but now looking back,

I know why he sometimes asked me for more, particularly the time near the Chinese New Year. But take a look at me now. What do I get from my charitable act? Have I made a better future? *Yes,* for him, but for myself? Definitely *no*. I don't know why I gave up my youth for someone's future. Can you tell me why?"

It became clear to Margaret why he was so sensitive and emotional every time he talked about his hardships in life. To show her understanding, she put her hand on his, giving it a gentle pat.

"Now, I am broke and have nothing, nothing at all. When I return to Hong Kong, I will have to start all over again. Tell me why I'm so stupid. Why did I believe his words? See how pathetic my life is? What am I now?"

Not sure if he wanted to hear this, Margaret said in her timid way, "I think you've become a better person."

Dominic gave a most unexpected response by congratulating himself on this achievement. "Yes, I've become a better person, much kinder and more caring. Let's drink to this new human being, a good person, a new me."

Margaret had no choice but to drink another glass. No sooner had she finished than Dominic started pouring another one for each of them.

Other than taking a short break when Margaret did the dishes and took care of Bei-bei's daily routine, they continued with their conversation. Dominic decided that they were done with his history and shifted the focus on Margaret's life in Canada. To do justice to Margaret's past seven and a half years, there was a good amount of wine and snacks in stock. By one in the morning, they were halfway through the third bottle, most of which was consumed by Dominic, who was then rather drunk. Like many drunken men who behaved in a way that was in contrast of their usual pattern, Dominic kept talking to himself and occasionally to Margaret, pacing from the kitchen to the living room in a hypnotic manner.

Margaret was by this time seated on a single sofa, listening to Dominic's monologue and the strong gusts of wind howling outside. What a duet—he raised both voice and pitch to match the sound of the wind as it grew louder! Dominic had a special pattern of pacing himself. He would be pacing back and forth from the kitchen to the living room, waving his arms when he was recalling a particular event. Sometimes he stopped moving his body in mid-sentence as he was searching for words to express his thoughts. When his memory came back, he would then circle around the dining table while recounting his experiences in detail. Having watched him for some time, Margaret felt a little dizzy, so she stopped looking at him and instead just listened and stared at the flower vase in front of her.

Though completely incoherent, Margaret could somehow piece together what had happened in her friend's life over the last few years. In that fateful summer when she was busy dating Nathan, Dominic had been actively joining a number of protest marches and gatherings in Victoria Park. It all started with his concern for the students and his disgust for his friends' indifference. To show that he wasn't just someone who cared about his own life, he went to his first march, then a meeting, then another one until he became a regular. Finally, he became so involved that he even got to know the organisers, who later entrusted an important task to him, in which Margaret also played a part. The memories slowly flashed back. What did not make sense before became clear to her now. Yang was no ordinary student from China; he was a student activist. He somehow managed to escape, although Dominic was unwilling to give away every single detail.

Having continuously talked for an hour, Dominic finally stopped, out of a sense of hopelessness rather than fatigue. Sitting on the sofa next to Margaret, he collapsed and broke down in great sobs. "We were both in love, you with Nathan, and me with Yang."

Now, with nobody talking, the sound of the wind became more noticeable. Was she imagining it, or was the wind trying to give its response?

Margaret was now sitting next to Dominic, who was still crying. Unlike Nathan, who cried until his face was all blotchy,

Dominic quietly let his tears roll down his cheeks. Directing his face with both her hands, Margaret was looking at her friend, studying his face like she had never done before. She first kissed him on his forehead, then his eyes, one by one, his cheeks and finally on his mouth.

The wind had finally quieted down, thus giving the living room a new silence. No, it wasn't completely silent, but a peaceful moment when Margaret only heard her own breathing and that of Dominic's, both of which synchronised with the background music from the radio. If the wind had not died down, she would have forgotten that the radio was still on, now playing the first movement of Beethoven's "Moonlight Sonata." Oh, how soothing and sublime it was to indulge in this dreamy state before the arrival of the stormy passages in the last movement.

It was some time before Dominic finally calmed down. His tears had dried too.

"It's late. Let's go to bed," said Margaret.

***

They did not talk much the day after. In fact, they slept so late that in their few waking hours they only had brief encounters in the kitchen, where they ate separately. They did not eat together. After a night of eating, drinking, and talking, they both needed some time on their own to detoxify their bodies and clear their minds.

Two more days passed before Dominic received his brother's phone call from Hong Kong, telling him that he had changed his mind. He would, after all, send his brother some money, for he wouldn't want to see him live like a leech, taking advantage of his friend's hospitality. Besides, it wouldn't be long before his tourist visa expired. Because of his brotherly love for him, he didn't want Dominic to be stranded in a foreign country.

When Dominic repeated his brother's words, Margaret comforted him and said, "It's no burden at all. You can apply to extend your visa. Then, you can stay here for as long as you want to."

Dominic remained obstinate about his departure and wouldn't listen to any alternative solutions. He seemed to have decided to give up on Canada as well as his unrequited love for Yang. Of course, Margaret did not argue with him and continued to play a good hostess until the money arrived. When it finally did, another week passed without them noticing how quickly time had flown.

Margaret drove him to the airport and said a hasty goodbye, in the hope that she would drive home safely before the roads were closed. She had been so busy hosting her friend in the last few weeks that she didn't watch much TV. Although she could tell the weather was unusually wet and warm for that time of the year, she had no idea that Manitoba was experiencing the flood of the century. Only when they listened to the radio on the way to the airport did Margaret get to know the seriousness of the situation. Hearing the news for the first time, she panicked.

"Stay in the car. I can handle it myself," said Dominic as he was unloading his luggage from the trunk. "Don't mind me. You'd better drive back as quickly as you can."

"I think I'll do that. Sorry that I can't stay with you much longer." Margaret stuck her head out of the window and pecked her friend on the cheek.

Just when Margaret was about to start her car, Dominic stopped her. "Wait, I think you deserve to know this. Yang is getting married in the summer to one of his female students in the university. It's a big slap in my face."

Out of all possible responses, Margaret replied rather clumsily, "Okay." They held hands for the last time. Holding his hands in hers in this final moment before his departure, it was as though Margaret had known this friend for all her life. She understood his sorrows, and she felt for him.

"Write to me when you are back," said Margaret.

"I will. Thank you for taking care of me," said Dominic.

"You're most welcome." Suddenly, the sky turned very dark with a heavy overcast. A nasty blizzard was imminent. "Go inside before you get soaked. Call me if your flight is delayed or cancelled, okay?"

There was no delay in Dominic's flight, fortunately, but Margaret's car journey took longer than usual because of a few road diversions. By the time she arrived home, both mistress and dog were starving. Rather than tending to her canine friend, Margaret's priority was to make sure that the house was all right. Thank God that their house was nowhere close to the Red River, so after a thorough check, Margaret felt assured that she was safe for the moment.

As soon as she gave herself and Bei-bei a quick meal, she called Brent to see if he was all right. No one picked up the call. Wondering where he could have gone when schools and offices were closed, Margaret made another phone call to Carol.

THE FLOOD

Happily recounting to Carol about Dominic's visit, Margaret wasn't aware that Brent had come over to check on her as she was driving home from the airport. She wasn't home in time to answer the door. For fifteen minutes, Brent received no response other than the whining sounds from Bei-bei. He left reluctantly with a troubled mind, wondering where Margaret had gone.

The roads in the first few kilometres were clear, and Brent had no problem navigating them until it started snowing. It was more like sleet than anything else. When visibility was reduced to no more than a few metres ahead, he made a wrong decision. Rather than pulling his car to the side, waiting for the storm to pass, he stubbornly drove on. It was too late when a warning sign was in sight, for his car had already turned into a flooded area.

Very soon, he was forced to stop his car when it refused to move any further. Unwillingly, he opened the door to see how he could get out of his predicament. The fact that the engine was still running was deceptive. With pretty much half his car mired in the snow, it took a while to get himself free. When he finally did, his legs submerged in half-melted snow. Frantically, he abandoned his car and ran to the nearest house. He banged at the door of a few houses before someone finally let him in. It was an old Indian woman who insisted that her home was safely sandbagged and refused to leave. She was one of the few residents who had stayed put and let nature take its course.

"It's my grandfather's house. I've been living here since I was born. I will protect it even if I have to die here." This was the greeting Brent received from the stubborn old woman, who gave him not only warm food and drink, but also a shelter for the night. Although he was glad to have an old soul guarding the area, without whom he would have frozen to death, he wondered why her house was so cold.

"All the power lines were destroyed in the storm. I'm running my kitchen with the last tank of gas," said his hostess. "I'm sure the water will recede in the next couple of days."

"How do you know?" asked Brent.

"I just do." She then added, "From experience."

It was a two-storey house. For their peace of mind, they abandoned the first floor that might submerge in icy water in the middle of the night. The old woman slept on the second floor, and Brent in the attic. It was freezing when Brent entered his small room. Having taken off his wet trousers and pulling two duvets filled with goose down over his head, Brent could just feel warm enough to manage a few hours of sleep. He wondered when he would see Margaret again. Oh well, shouldn't he be glad to have his life saved?

When Brent opened his eyes at the first light of dawn, he wondered if he had slept at all. His eyelids felt heavy and gluey; his cheeks that had been well-covered during the night were still cold; and worst of all, his limbs that spread on the mattress were lifelessly freezing and aching. It was true that the mattress was so old that its springs no longer functioned. Rather than supporting the weight of any sleeper, they pierced upward into one's flesh and bone. The few springs that still worked did so in the most illogical way. With only a thin layer of foam that stubbornly refused to go, it was torture to sleep on it even for a few hours. But Brent was quite certain that this bed had nothing to do with his body condition. He had slept in worse beds, or no bed at all while camping, and nothing like this had ever happened. It had to be a fever. He knew he was running a bad one, but he was too weak to move. With no other choice, he lay there with his eyes half closed, hoping that his hostess would come and check on him. When she finally did, Brent had gone back into his half-sleep state. She came in without knocking on the door, or she might have done so without Brent hearing it.

"Morning, I hope you had a good night's sleep. It hasn't stopped raining, but I might be able to go out and get some help for you. Where did you say you left your car?"

Brent struggled to open his eyes or say something in return without success. All he managed was a grunt.

"What's wrong with you?" The woman came over to the bedside and put her rough hand on Brent's forehead. "Oh, goodness me, you are burning."

On hearing the cue, Brent no longer felt cold. Instead, it seemed as if his whole body were on fire. A slight touch anywhere on his skin hurt him. He felt intense pain all over his body as the woman busied herself changing his clothes, undershirt, and bedsheet. She then rubbed some ointment on his shoulders and chest. Brent would normally reject any alternative remedy without understanding its implication, but now he had no energy to protest.

When Brent was changed into some loose, oversized pyjamas, the woman sat him up on the bed and brought some water to his mouth.

"You'd better hydrate yourself. I don't suppose you want to eat anything, but maybe some soup will do?"

Brent wanted to thank her, but no sound came out from his mouth.

"That's okay. You'll get some rest now. When you are feeling better, I'll ask you for your full name. Not that anything will happen to you, but in case anyone wonders why a white man's staying in my house, I have an answer." The woman might have said more, but Brent became unconscious with sleep again.

Brent had never been so sick before. This experience certainly made him realise how fragile human lives were. In delirium, he could just vaguely make sense of what was happening around him. He was fed a few times a day, a soupy liquid that was usually tasteless but sometimes carried a pungent smell. Before he knew it, there was a fire burning that made the temperature of his attic room a lot more bearable. The warmth from his daily nourishment and the fire kept up his spirits. He nearly forgot that he hadn't seen Margaret for days, or even weeks, something that he couldn't be sure of.

His sense of time and space were first blurred by a high fever, then later a repetitive pattern of eating and sleeping. Since when there was a pot cooking above the fire, Brent had no idea. Before he knew it, the room was turned into a makeshift kitchen, so food was within easy reach for him and the old woman. She was now spending more time in the attic, probably because this was the only place in the whole house that was habitable.

In the disguise of peace and quiet, Brent was once woken up by a loud noise downstairs. He first thought that there was an explosion. In response to his urgent shouts, his hostess assured him that everything was fine, but rather than showing her face, the old woman set herself to work for an hour or so somewhere in the house. All he could hear was more noise—first a big thump that shook the whole house, then the sound of hammering and sawing that would have been extremely annoying to a healthy person. But with his nose and ears blocked, it sounded like waves in the ocean. Very soon, he went back to sleep.

When Brent opened his eyes again, it was dark and still raining outside. The old woman was sitting next to the fire with one hand resting on the arm of her chair and the other stirring something in the pot. It was just bright enough for Brent to make out her features from the side. She had a double chin and a flat, big nose. The boils on her face and neck were hideously oversized. But rather than finding it grotesque, Brent admired this image in front of his eyes as though he were viewing a painting in a gallery. This woman had a face that glowed in the dark. One of her hands was making regular movements in circles until it got tired and stopped.

Watching this image had such a calming effect on Brent that a low cry from the old woman caused him no alarm.

"I must have dozed off. The soup nearly burnt," cried the old woman. "Now, come, you should be strong enough to eat by yourself." She filled a bowl and passed it to Brent.

As he was eating, the old woman put a few more logs into the fire.

"Are you not eating?" asked Brent.

"I will, but not now, maybe later." She continued tending the fire.

"There's a good supply of wood?" said Brent.

"Sure there is."

"There seems to be a trademark on the one that you've just put in," said Brent out of curiosity.

Forking it with a poker, she gave a good look at the piece in the cracking fire and said matter-of-factly, "Do you mean this one? Oh, it's one of the doors of my favourite kitchen cabinet."

Brent stopped eating and looked at her, not being sure whether he was supposed to say anything.

"Stop giving me that look," said the old woman.

"I'm sorry," said Brent apologetically.

"What are you sorry for? Making a fire just for myself is a luxury, but for two people and that you are so sick? It's worth the while."

"Thank you. Do you think the power will be back soon?"

"Maybe, maybe not. How do I know? The phone stopped working. My last tank of gas is finished, and now we are stranded with only a few days of food left. I know nothing anymore. God help us!"

"The soup is good. Can I have some more, please?"

"Sure you can. It's the first time you've liked my cooking. You were so sick the last few days."

"How long have I been staying in your place?"

"Let me see. You came on Friday night. What day is today? Tuesday or Wednesday? It may be Thursday. Anyway, my safe bet is something like five or six days."

"And you stayed here with me all the time?" Brent took his second bowl of soup from his hostess.

"What do you mean by staying with you? This is my house."

"I know, but you could have gone away, leaving me here."

"Why would I do that? Why would I leave you to die in my house? Your spirit does not belong here."

"Oh, I hadn't thought about that. What I meant was that you don't have to look after me."

"We are a generous people. Anyone who comes to our place, we will take him in and give him food and shelter. We did the same for many generations in the past and will for many more generations to come. We haven't changed much."

In all the years of studying and working in Winnipeg, Brent almost never made friends with the indigenous people. Once in a while, he would meet one in class, but he almost never socialised with them. His knowledge of them was confined to that given in the history books. What the woman had said made him realise how little he knew about them.

"What's your name?" Brent asked.

"Tell me your name first."

"My name is Brent Owen."

"Mine is Keetah."

"I like the sound of your name."

"Thank you. I like the sound of yours too." After a short pause, Keetah said, "Why don't you go to sleep now? I think you will be strong enough to help me with the sandbags tomorrow."

"What about you? Aren't you going to sleep?"

"I'll stay in my chair, keeping an eye on the fire and the rain."

"How can I sleep when you are not eating or resting?"

"Don't worry about me. I will get some food and some rest, eventually."

No matter how much Brent wanted to stay awake to keep her company, he failed as soon as his head hit the pillow.

The following day presented itself as a big challenge, not because Brent hadn't recovered, and he sure did, but he hadn't thought how much work was required in the present conditions. How Keetah kept everything in check in the last few days all by herself was beyond his comprehension. Not only were they safe from the floods as long as they stayed in the attic, Keetah managed to keep the fire going and feed both of them with nutritious food. There wasn't a lot, but surely enough to keep them going.

As he was descending the stairs on his wobbly legs for the first time upon his recovery, Brent numbered his steps by mentally charting the watermarks on the wall. He was amazed that one of them leveled with the last step of the staircase, just below the landing to his attic room.

"Did the water come up this high?" asked Brent.

"You bet," said Keetah. "Go down and you will see it for yourself."

What awaited him was a sorry and frightful sight. Walking on the floor that was still carpeted produced squishy noises. On the parts where the carpet was peeled off, Brent had to walk into puddles of water, some of them deep enough to serve as a basin for baby baths. Children wearing rain boots would find this house a wonderful playground to splash around in. To contain the damage to a minimum, Keetah decided to give up the rear of her house, which was why the kitchen was the worst-hit area, with water levels reaching as high as her knees. Running out of sandbags, Keetah decided to use the last few to draw a line of demarcation, marking a safe zone for herself and Brent. What made her decide to give up on the kitchen was anybody's guess. Now standing on the last step of his descent, Brent could see how messy the kitchen was. A few objects, some looked like Tupperware, were floating as though they had been set free and were enjoying their newfound freedom. Plates and kitchen utensils were lying everywhere. The only traces left behind that hinted an existence of a kitchen cabinet before were its knobs and glass doors.

"What do you want me to do now?" Brent couldn't help asking.

"We have no choice but to make more sandbags," said Keetah, "until someone comes to save us."

"But how?"

"I'll show you. Look at me."

Taking him to the workshop where Keetah had slept for a few nights, they both set to work immediately. Keetah started working on her sewing machine, resizing what used to be bedsheets into squares to imitate the look of cushion covers.

She passed one to Brent and said, "Now I want you to fill it with whatever you can find in my drawers. Choose cotton and anything that is absorbent. Skip nylon. When you are done, pass it back to me and I'll sew it up."

No sooner had Brent started working did he ask, mainly for the sake of saying something, "How many of these have you made so far?"

"Cut it out and just focus on your work."

Brent said no more after that. For the whole morning, Keetah and he must have made dozens of amateur sandbags, filling them with shreds of cloth or any material that they thought would work. While Keetah was in charge of the production and did not leave the workshop, Brent was ordered to carry them to the different parts of the house. There he would replace the old ones that were soaked wet with newly handmade cloth bags.

When the bathtub had run out of space for storing any more used sandbags, Brent asked, "Where do you want me to put these?"

"Don't bring them here! Take them away, anywhere but here. Can't you see we have to keep this room dry?" Another of Brent's innocent question was met with a stern rebuke.

Keetah seemed a different person at work. The gentle and caring nurse turned herself into a working monster, swearing at her sewing machine with fire and fury. Seeing no end to this disaster, Brent could feel her frustration. Keetah could be wrong to think that the water level would soon recede.

Brent had learned his lesson and dared not disturb Keetah, even though he was utterly worn out and his stomach was giving him away by making annoying rumblings.

"Why don't you go upstairs and see what you can make for lunch?" said Keetah with a frown.

Brent gingerly left the room, as if by doing so he appeared unwilling to abandon his work and his comrade. The fact was that his body desperately needed to replenish as well as discharge some liquid. They hadn't stopped working for four hours, and Keetah was still going.

Now back in his attic room, it didn't take long before Brent decided what to do. With no one tending a fire in the last few hours, the room temperature had drastically dropped. He needed to start a fire for keeping the room warm as well as heating up the soup. There wasn't much food left. All he could put in would be a few pieces of potato left on the chopping board. The soup was by now watered down to a thin liquid. To make it edible, he would have to add salt and pepper, which was still aplenty.

Once he set to work in this kitchen/bedroom, he found it surprisingly calming. The hectic pace of work in the morning was now reduced to simple motions of stirring and watching the rain outside. Against all logic, it didn't bother him that the rain hadn't stopped. Although he should really consider leaving the house, knowing that sooner or later the water level would rise again, the thing was that Keetah seemed to have passed her stubbornness onto him. He wanted to stay with his hostess through thick and thin, and he didn't care if this way of returning thanks was absurd.

Checking the rain from the corner of his eye, something caught his attention. Was it a dream, or was his imagination playing a trick on him? He saw an army of rescuers marching in their direction, and it looked like they would soon arrive at their door. This was a moment he couldn't afford to miss. He had to catch their attention. Before he knew it, he was shouting and waving a spatula from a small attic window. When no one seemed to have noticed him, Brent hit on anything he could get hold of. He kept hitting the pan and banging on the wall.

"Give me a break. What are you doing up there?" Keetah yelled from downstairs. Her voice was certainly more powerful than all the noises that Brent had produced. It captured someone from the crowd, who tuned her head and saw Brent frantically moving his arms with his right hand still holding the spatula as though it were a heavy flag.

Brent hurried downstairs and opened the front door to welcome the rescuers. "Come, Keetah. We are at last saved." Brent was so overwhelmed with emotion that his own words almost choked him.

"What makes you think I want to leave?"

"But you must. It's not safe here anymore."

"You go where you like. I'm staying."

A big team of rescuers were by now standing by the door, some of them carrying bundles of ropes and others with shovels over their shoulders. Among them were both professionals and volunteers. Even though they were impressed with this novel ad hoc sandbagging operation, they insisted on an immediate evacuation. This turned out to be an almost impossible task. Keetah just wouldn't listen to them.

As they were arguing what to do, Brent, who had already left the house, now came back to check what the commotion was all about.

"We must evacuate everyone and reduce losses the best we can," someone in the crowd said.

"You are her friend, right? Can you persuade her to leave? The house is not safe," said a man who appeared to be the group leader.

Having recovered from what could possibly be pneumonia by taking Keetah's traditional remedy, Brent was no longer sure if the house was really unsafe.

"I am not exactly her friend, but she did more than a lot of my friends would have done for me in the past few days. My car stopped running and I got stuck here. If not for Keetah, who refused to leave her place, I would have frozen to death. I wasn't able to get out of bed because of a bad flu. It's my hostess who looked after me and kept me warm. I didn't even realise the lower floor was half flooded. I slept well and rested in peace. There wasn't a single moment I felt unsafe. Keetah was full of energy, and I think she had the power to protect her house. Besides, she has a good reason for staying."

"What's her reason?" someone asked.

"I think she's guarding her place or guarding the spirits of her ancestors. She mentioned something like that to me, though I'm not sure what she meant. Anyway, we shall perhaps respect her way of dealing with nature."

After some negotiation, the officer in charge finally made his decision. The rescue team would ensure that there were enough volunteers to monitor the water level for as long as Keetah chose to remain in the house. They couldn't really argue with a woman who placed the importance of protecting her ancestors' sacred land over her own life, could they?

Within an hour or so, more volunteers arrived, most likely from the vicinity of the affected area. They looked young and eager, although they didn't seem to have much physical strength. *Were they college students?* Brent wondered. *And would they do?*

Almost immediately, Brent changed his role from that of a lodger to a volunteer. To return the favour, Brent had to watch the water level more closely than anybody else. He felt so indebted to Keetah that he made it his duty to take charge of the squad. For an hour or so, Brent kept running around to get a big picture. Once he spotted a high-risk area, he would designate extra hands to ensure it was sufficiently sandbagged. It was a tiring job, but Brent was glad that he recovered and was fit to make a contribution. The officer in charge was relieved for Brent to take control. Suddenly, they both sensed that the water level was about to rise.

A group of young volunteers arrived just in time before the situation got out of hand. For a few minutes no one dared to speak, let alone joke. All they did was keep passing sandbags from one hand to another, with a single hope of stopping the floods and to minimise damage. When the critical moment passed, everyone exclaimed in relief. As soon as someone said "whew," another person joined in, and then another one until everyone had a go.

The volunteers had to be really tired by now. Seeing that there was no immediate danger, someone, probably the same person who started the "whew" game, started another one. This time, he made an introduction of himself, "Simon Knowles, Alberta."

"Diana Fraser, Edmonton," said the person next to him.

"Victoria Smith, Winnipeg," then said the next one.

"Kurt Tremblay, Winnipeg."

The young people just went on with the chain introductions for a while, and they seemed to have a lot of fun doing this. *Definitely college students*, thought Brent. He wasn't paying too much attention to their game until he heard a name familiar to his ear.

"Carol Murphy, Winnipeg."

"Margaret Young, Winnipeg."

At first, Brent didn't trust he heard it right. He turned in the direction of the voice and looked for that face, the face of his life, that he'd been missing for so long. When he spotted his love, he ran in a frenzy, forgetting to take a crisscross path to avoid water puddles. As soon as he reached Margaret, Brent held her tightly in his arms, refusing to let go.

As they worked side by side on the following few days, Brent and Margaret each recounted their experiences. Extremely worried about Brent's disappearance, Margaret had even once wondered if he got killed in an accident. Anything could happen in a disaster. To take her mind off the worry, she finally agreed to work as a volunteer under Carol's persuasion. A few hours of manual work every day helped her sleep much better.

"Brent might have gone to check on his aunt." Carol had tried her best to comfort her friend.

It *was* possible that Brent had driven to Brandon to make sure his aunt was safe, but even so, he would have let her know, unless telecommunications in the area broke down. Margaret kept telling herself that this had to be the reason, or she would have gone crazy.

It was such a relief to see Brent again that Margaret completely forgot about all the fights they had before. Margaret understood that there had to be rough patches for anyone who was in love. She was convinced of her love for Brent, or she wouldn't have felt so worried in the days when he went missing. She was happy to be involved in this rescue operation and be able to work closely with the man she loved.

After a few days of intense work, Keetah's neighbourhood was finally declared safe. The officer in charge decided that his team and the relief workers could handle the situation by themselves without the help of the volunteers. Brent and Margaret discussed what they should do. It wasn't easy for Brent to leave the woman who saved his life.

"I left Bei-bei with my neighbour. I'll have to go home and check on her and the house," said Margaret.

"I'll go with you," said Brent.

"Are you sure? I mean, you can stay and help Keetah clean up her place."

"No, I'll go with you. I can come back later," said Brent.

Taking Margaret to say goodbye to Keetah, Brent didn't expect other volunteers to follow suit. The house was suddenly packed with young, sweaty people.

"I come to say thank you and goodbye, Keetah," said Brent.

"Oh, you're welcome." She said after a pause, "What do you thank me for?"

"I thank you for your hospitality, your generosity, and your kindness."

"I didn't know I have so many virtues."

"Yes, you do. And I won't forget you."

"Come and visit me." Seeing that he was holding hands with Margaret, she added, "With your wife."

"My girlfriend," said Brent with a smile, feeling embarrassed by Keetah's blunder.

"Wife," repeated Keetah. She then added, "Soon to be."

"Uh?"

"Ask for her hand," said Keetah.

Brent couldn't quite make out what she had said until someone in the crowd cheered, "Yeah, propose to her."

Having done mass games a number of times, this crowd was fast to pick up the cue. It wasn't long before everyone was chanting, "Propose. Propose. Propose."

"I would if had a ring, but I don't have one," said Brent.

In high spirits, everyone was so busy laughing and joking that no one noticed Keetah's brief absence. When she joined the crowd again, she put something in Brent's hand, "Put this on her finger. I think my mother's ring will do."

It wasn't exactly a life-and-death experience, but the last ten days did create a fear in both their minds. They didn't want to be separated again, so getting married seemed the most natural course in life in times of a natural disaster. There were now so many people that those at the back were jostling to get a better view. All were eager to witness a happy moment.

"But I can't take your mother's gift from you," said Brent soon after he had slipped the ring onto Margaret's finger.

"Of course you can. I have many of the same style. Do you think I would give it to you if she only gave me one?"

Everybody laughed. It was an unexpectedly joyous moment. Margaret felt that she was the luckiest girl in the world, though only if it could last.

In the same instance on the other side of the globe, however, marked an entirely different moment—one that was rather disturbing. There was a lot of water too.

Wasn't it funny that everything tasted and smelt like salt? one wondered. Where did the water come from? Was it going to stop? Not likely. Water slowly seeped through every single pore in the skin, and it felt ticklish. If only one could giggle in a matter of life and death.

Hold it, please. Don't let it happen too fast. Let's capture this moment. Let's enjoy the flashbacks of life while the head is still clear.

PART V
AUGUST 2008
BEIJING

Who controls the past controls the future: who controls the present controls the past.

—George Orwell, *1984*

AN OPENING CEREMONY

"You are late."

"Yes, but only fifteen minutes."

"Still, you are late. How did you get in?"

"I can always find a way," said Margaret cheekily as she was about to sit down. Hugging her father and kissing him on his forehead, she turned to him and said, "Hi, Dad. Sorry that I'm late. What have I missed?"

"Nothing much."

"Oh, it's hot here," said Margaret.

"Now, take this and shut up."

In less than a minute since her arrival at the Bird's Nest, where the opening ceremony of the Olympic Games took place, Margaret received her mother's second reprimand. To make sure that Margaret made no more fuss, she passed a yellow fan to her husband, who then passed it on to their daughter.

It helped a little, but not much. It was really hot in the Bird's Nest. Summer nights in Beijing in the open air were unbearably hot for Margaret, who had spent her last four summers in air-conditioned hotels and restaurants. As she was fanning herself, she noticed that some guests were doing the same, holding a fan of the same style. It had to be a souvenir from the organising committee.

The fact that not everyone was fanning themselves made Margaret wonder if it was considered impolite to do so. To play it safe, she brought her hand to a stop, just in case someone was watching. After all, she didn't come to only watch the Games. In the coming week, her parents would connect her with all the important people they knew so that she could extend her business projects in the capital city. For them to get seats to watch this important event, Margaret's parents had to work their way through. Moving out of Hong Kong did not cause them to break old ties. They understood the importance of showing up at social events, making appearances at parties, wedding banquets, and funerals so that people wouldn't forget them. *Quanxi*, or connections, were extremely important to help secure any business project, especially the lucrative ones, in China.

Looking around to see if there was anything interesting going on, Margaret saw someone about five or six rows in front of them turn to wave and smile at her.

"Who is he?" whispered Margaret. She smiled back as a way to show politeness.

"Mr. Chen's son, Harry. Remember? We met the family at the airport yesterday," said her father.

"I don't remember seeing him or his family. There were too many people."

"We are having lunch with them tomorrow."

"Are we?"

"Yes, we are."

"Oh no, I can't. I'll be meeting Kate tomorrow at the airport."

"Can you ask Carol to go instead?"

"But Carol doesn't speak Putonghua. If anything happens, she can't handle it."

"Neither can you," said her father.

"I can at least speak Cantonese and read some Chinese."

"I'll see if I can send someone to meet Kate at the airport. You must show up for lunch if you want to do business in Beijing. Mr. Chen knows all the restaurant owners here."

"Really? Does he? Harry or his father?"

"Both of them."

Seeing that the opening performances were about to begin, they dropped their conversation. A girl of about five years old went onto the stage, singing a song that everyone in the local audience seemed to know and sang along. From a distance, all Margaret could see was her red dress and two ponytails, one on each side. A very cute little girl. Singing with her were other children of different ages who were dressed in costumes that represented different ethnic minorities in China. They were holding hands and walking from one end of the stage to the other. The girl in the red dress remained on the stage and sang in a voice that sounded rather too mature for someone of her age. If she was older than she appeared, Margaret couldn't tell.

There was more singing after the children's choir, and it was a part that everyone had to participate in—the singing of the national anthem. Although Margaret couldn't sing along, she knew the melody quite well. As soon as she recognised the music, she stood up promptly, and her face suddenly looked solemn. Margaret figured that she should make up for what she wasn't able to do with at least the right facial expression. She seemed to have done the right thing—even her mother turned and nodded at her approvingly. And why not, if the hosts were that easy to please? Who could tell that what Margaret most wanted now was a drink with Carol?

The audience was then rewarded with visual enjoyment, first a fireworks display and then a dance performance combined with the art of Chinese calligraphy. That had to be Margaret's favourite. She had never seen anything like it before. After watching a short film about the history of paper making, the Bird's Nest was plunged into darkness. Then, being shone by a spotlight, a giant scroll of paper appeared, first rolled up and then slowly unfolding itself. In the background, Margaret could hear the sound of a Chinese musical instrument, probably a *guqin*.

In the middle of the scroll was a white canvas that took up pretty much all the space at centre stage. The first dancer slowly emerged and started making elegant body movements on the white canvas. Each time his hands touched the canvas, he made a stroke and left a trail of ink. He must have had a brush hidden somewhere in his sleeves. After the solo, other dancers joined him, performing in twos and threes. They all left trails as their bodies slid smoothly and glided effortlessly on the canvas. Both their body movements and the trails they left behind on the canvas were amazing. It was wonderful to watch these dancers, all dressed in black, moving on a white backdrop. The pattern they made on the canvas was no accident; it had to be a result of hours of labourious practice and trial and error. After the last dancer left the mark of what represented the sun in one stroke, the painting was complete and was lifted into the air for the audience to admire.

Margaret enjoyed the performance so much that what came afterwards seemed redundant, almost superfluous. She quickly lost interest and started fanning again. Fifteen more minutes into the ceremony, she could bear it no more and began sending messages on her phone.

"Stop that, your mom says," said her father softly in her ear.

"I have to stop anyway. The reception is really bad here," said Margaret. "I thought they were supposed to go easy with censorship."

With nothing to do, Margaret diverted her attention back to the stage and noticed a pair of eyes staring in her direction.

"What is he watching me for, Dad?"

"He must find you attractive."

"I don't mean Harry. It's someone sitting close to his group."

"Oh, that. I don't recognise him; he's perhaps some friend of the Chens."

"But why is he so rude, staring at me like that?"

"That's not what he thinks though."

"What does he think then?"

"He's just curious."

"About what?"

"Probably that Harry has some foreign friends."

"I'm not a foreigner. I live in Hong Kong."

"We are all foreigners here."

Tapping lightly on her husband's shoulder with her fan, Betty said, "Will the two of you stop talking and watch the ceremony?"

A reprimand would be imminent at the slightest provocation. Margaret decided that she had better not cross the line. So, what could she do now? It would still be a while before the athletes' teams entered the hall to greet the audience. She had only one option: keep quiet and make some mental plan for the rest of the night. At the right moment, she would make an excuse to leave and join Carol, who must be waiting anxiously for her in the hotel bar. She felt bad for leaving her friend behind. But what could she do when her parents insisted that they didn't manage to get another ticket for Carol?

Margaret couldn't wait to do some girl talk over a drink or two with her old buddy. The last time she made a short visit to Canada and saw Carol was well over a year ago. It wasn't just work that'd been keeping her in Hong Kong; it was her divorce with Brent. She couldn't bring herself back to the place more often than necessary. Even though most of their married years were spent outside Canada, she still got emotional every time she went home. Perhaps it mattered more to Margaret how their relationship started, and the country reminded her too much of that.

Her quiet thoughts were interrupted every time Harry and his friend turned to look at her. When their occasional glances became more frequent and intense, Margaret started to feel uneasy. Of all the men she knew, no one behaved like them. This kind of social, or anti-social, behaviour was both new and different to what Margaret was used to. It was rude of them for not even trying to pretend; they should at least make an effort to hide their curiosity. Making a good effort was what Margaret did. No matter how uncomfortable she was in her suit, she wore it, just to ensure that she was properly dressed for the occasion. All her sexy party clothes were stored in the hotel wardrobe for the latter part of the trip. Margaret wondered why they couldn't do the same. If she had the sense to try and blend into the local community, shouldn't her host make her feel more welcome too?

Finally, when the athletes from the different countries made their parade, it was already nine thirty. Margaret was getting so impatient that even her dad knew that she had some other plan in mind. Having sat down for an hour and a half, the audience was by now getting tired. Some of them took the chance to stretch their legs when they saw their country's athletes marching into the stadium. People waved and cheered as their fellow sportsmen waved back and took pictures and videos of the audience.

Greece came to greet the audience first, and why not. It was, after all, where the Olympic Games started. It took each team a few minutes to make a full circle of the stadium while the audience on each side had a quick glance of them. Margaret saw many teams marching past her—Guinea, Guinea-Bissau, Turkey, Turkmenistan, Maldives, and many others—but still no sign of Canada. Before she started feeling bored again, she was saved by an incoming text: "Are you coming now?"

"Not yet, still no sign of the Canadian team," Margaret wrote back.

"Hurry up, I'm on my third."

"Won't be long. Take it easy."

"I'll try, but very hard. Nobody to talk to."

"I can see them coming now. Yes, it's our team. I'll leave soon. Just wait."

"Okay."

Margaret and her parents stood up to wave at the team, cheering and smiling at them. Seeing that Margaret was wearing a suit in red and white, her dad said, "Good match with the flag."

"Thank you," said Margaret. As the Canadian athletes were walking further away from them, she continued to say, "Dad, I have to leave after this. Carol's waiting for me at the hotel."

"All right. Ask a volunteer to help you get a taxi. I'll see you tomorrow morning at breakfast. What time is Kate flying in?"

"Two in the afternoon."

"Good, plenty of time to arrange pick-up."

Her watch showed ten thirty in the taxi. If the volunteer had not insisted on getting a taxi at the other gate, she would have arrived at the hotel and been sipping cocktail with Carol by now. With his local knowledge, he knew that it would be a much shorter distance, and hence cheaper, if Margaret took a taxi at the south gate.

"I don't mind paying more. I want to be there soon."

"Come with me. It's only a short walk," said the volunteer.

It turned out to be a challenge for someone wearing a suit and high heels. Making apologies along the way didn't help much; the volunteer made Margaret exercise so much that she was completely soaked with sweat when she got into the taxi.

"Sorry for the long walk. I hope you enjoyed the opening ceremony," said the volunteer.

"Yes, I did. It was marvellous," said Margaret before the taxi drove away.

Probably because everyone was still watching the ceremony, the roads were almost empty with hardly any traffic. It turned out to be an extremely short ride of merely five minutes, which would usually take twenty or longer even during off-peak hours.

After saying hello to Carol, Margaret went up to her room for a quick shower. When she came to join her friend again, she looked refreshed in her one-piece black dress. It was a simple slip-on with a belt loosely tied at her waist. Wearing a small amount of jasmine fragrance, she smelt very nice too.

"I am sorry to keep you waiting," said Margaret as she was giving her friend a hug.

"You must tell me something interesting. I was watching the opening ceremony. It's all right with the visual effects, but I wish I could understand what they said," complained Carol.

Just when Margaret thought she had run away from the opening ceremony, there it was again right in front of her. Everyone in the bar was watching the huge flat screen mounted on the wall, sipping their drinks and talking excitedly about the event.

"Let's order our drinks first," said Margaret.

"I had four martinis already. I think I'll go for a juice now," said Carol.

"Good idea. I'll need water, plenty of it. I'm so thirsty," said Margaret.

"Why?"

"It's a long story. I'll tell you in a minute."

Margaret was a good storyteller. Although there wasn't much to tell about Harry and his friend, she managed to describe them in such great detail that Carol could almost picture them in her mind's eye.

"So, they also have the unruly hairstyle like the men over there," whispered Carol as she glanced over Margaret's shoulder.

"Yes, they do. You can't really tell where the parting begins or ends."

"And you are going to have lunch with them tomorrow?"

"I'm not sure if his friend will be there, and I hope he won't, but I will definitely have to sit through a boring lunch with Harry and his family."

"So what time are we going to see you?"

"Not sure. I'll text you as soon as I know."

"Are you sure I don't have to go and meet Kate at the airport?"

"You can go if you want to. What I meant was that my dad will arrange everything. He will get someone to go and pick her up from the airport. You can just relax here, maybe have a massage or a late breakfast. I hope we'll all meet for dinner later."

"Of course we will. You can't leave Kate and me here."

"Relax, I'll slip away as soon as I can," said Margaret.

"I came up with my bucket list. Make sure you help me tick off every single one of them."

"Tell me what you want to do."

Margaret listened and then safely concluded that they had more or less the same idea of having fun. Margaret had also planned for the three of them to go places of Carol's wish—other than the must-see tourist spots such as the Great Wall, the Forbidden City, and the Summer Palace, she had reserved half a day and a night in the Houhai bar area.

"What about the hutongs? I heard that to make way for building the infrastructure for the Olympic Games, a lot of hutongs were pulled down. I want to see those that still remain."

"We will see some of them on our way to the bar area," said Margaret.

So, that was the plan, which pleased Carol so much that she forgot the boredom she had experienced earlier. Now that Margaret had quenched her thirst, she ordered her first Martini.

"Do you want one?" asked Margaret.

"Nah, I'd better stick with non-alcoholic. Give me another orange juice, please."

"That's a good girl."

"I don't want a hangover in my first week," said Carol. "By the way, what's Houhai like?"

"It's great. You'll love it."

"Better than here?"

"Of course, much better," said Margaret.

"In what way?"

"In many different ways. For one thing, drinks are much cheaper. Customers are so much younger and more fun. The locals don't speak a lot of English, but you don't really mind. You can't make much of a conversation there anyway, except at break time. Most of the time, there's live music. It's very loud, and you can't even hear yourself."

"What sort of music do they play?"

"Rock, blues, and pop. There's a range. Of course, all in Putonghua."

"So why didn't we go there today?"

"I figured that I would be too tired after watching the opening ceremony."

"Come on, it can't be that tiring. You didn't even stay for the whole thing."

"True, but we can't go without Kate. It won't be the same without her. She speaks Putonghua and can explain things to us."

Their conversation was interrupted by a waiter who brought them their drinks. Margaret thanked and smiled at him before he walked away.

"Did you thank him in Cantonese?"

"No, I did it in Putonghua. Saying thank you is one of the few words I know in Putonghua."

"I thought the language is called Mandarin, isn't it?"

"I think both are fine, but people usually call it Putonghua now."

"Why?" asked Carol.

"Don't ask me why. I'm not an expert. I just know that although the city is now called Beijing, certain names don't change, things such as Peking University and Peking duck."

"Funny, isn't it?"

Taking a sip of their drink, they both turned their heads to the flat screen as a natural response to hearing a speech in English. It was Mr. Jacques Rogge, president of the International Olympic Committee.

"Mr. President of the People's Republic of China, Mr. Liu Qi, and members of the organising committee, dear Chinese friends, dear athletes, for a long time, China has dreamed of opening its doors and inviting the world's athletes to Beijing for the Olympic Games. Tonight, that dream comes true. Congratulations, Beijing [applause]. 祝賀北京 [applause]."

"Is that Putonghua?" asked Carol.

"Yes, as long as you speak a few words, people are impressed."

"Really? I shall perhaps learn a few phrases too."

"I'll teach you what I know later. Let's hear the speech first," said Margaret.

"You have chosen the theme of this game, 'One World, One Dream.' That is what we are tonight [applause]," continued Mr. Rogge.

"People like him, don't they?" Carol commented on the frequency of the applause.

"It's a typical way of showing appreciation in China," explained Margaret.

"Is that the same in Hong Kong?" asked Carol.

"No, I don't think so." She then added, "Anyway, it has a different culture."

"As one world, we grieve with you over the tragic earthquake in Sichuan Province. We were moved by the great courage and the solidarity of the Chinese people [applause]. As one dream, may this Olympic Games bring you joy, hope and pride [applause] . . . Our special thanks also go to the thousands of gracious volunteers, without whom none of this would be possible. Beijing, you are host to the present and the gateway to the future. Thank you. 感謝你. I now have the honour of asking the president of the People's Republic of China to open the games of the twenty-ninth Olympia of the modern era."

"Interruptions aside, it's still a good speech, isn't it?" said Carol.

"You think so? It's nothing but *Pai Ma Pi*," said Margaret.

"What does that mean?"

"Literally, it means 'stroking the horse's bottom.' What I mean is, his speech is nothing but flattery."

"Brilliant. I like the sound of the phrase. Say it again, please."

They stopped watching the opening ceremony after the speech and turned to making sounds, sometimes making up sounds that they thought were phrases in Putonghua. The customers at the table next to theirs and the waiter who served them were drawn close to these two beautiful foreign ladies. Very soon, nobody was watching the opening ceremony anymore; everyone, mostly Chinese men, volunteered to offer their language advice and suddenly made the bar into a classroom. There were not too many people in the bar, usually hotel residents staying there for the night. With a small intimate group and her good friend from Canada, Margaret finally relaxed her mind, not bothering to think about lunch with the Chen family tomorrow.

It had to be the lunch that Margaret would remember about this trip to Beijing in the years to come. She might not have much memory of the places she visited. Even the Tiananmen Square that Kate insisted on visiting was a blur to her. What remained in her memory was their disagreement in the itinerary.

"Let's skip it," Margaret remembered saying this to her friends. "Tiananmen Square is out of our way. To get there will take up too much of our time."

"But we must go and see the place where so many students gathered together in the hope of a better country," said Kate. "What do you say, Carol?"

"I am open. Anything is new to me." Carol gave her most politically correct reply.

"Please," pleaded Kate. "Think of all the young people who died for their belief in a better world."

Even though there wasn't much to see, other than Chairman Mao's photo and the guards, Margaret was glad that they went, or she would never be able to imagine the scale of the demonstration.

PEKING DUCK

Margaret had only a vague memory of Tiananmen Square, but she would never forget lunch with the Chen family. It was an elaborate meal; everything including food and drink, literally every single detail, right down to the seating arrangement, was planned. As someone who was not familiar with the way of doing business beyond Hong Kong, she wasn't aware that even a meal was part of a potential deal.

Mr. Chen sent his chauffeur to pick up Margaret and her parents from the hotel. A twenty-minute ride took them to a district that looked commercial but not quite up-market. The sedan stopped in front of a building where Harry and his friend were waiting to meet them. Margaret's heart sank at the sight of the same pair of eyes that closely watched her the night before. He introduced himself as Ma Qiang. They quickly walked into the building and took a lift that was only big enough for the five of them. A tight space either did wonders to human relationships or completely ruined them. Trapped in a tiny slow-moving cubicle, Margaret was given the chance to understand Harry's intentions. He showed off his knowledge of the place by talking non-stop on their way up, breathing out hot air on Margaret's neck as he was pronouncing his English words with enthusiasm.

"Here we are," said Ma Qiang as the door of the lift slowly opened. "Welcome. This is where you will eat the best Peking duck. All the bigwigs eat here."

As they were stepping out of the lift, Harry placed his hand on Margaret's waist and refused to let go. A simple gesture turned out to be rather annoying. As they were walking towards the private room, Margaret wondered how and where he had picked up this odd behaviour. She wanted to walk away but was afraid that it would be embarrassing. Apparently, he had to have picked up some Western mannerisms while he was studying overseas, but his half-learned etiquette made both of them look ridiculous.

"Guess who I have brought?" Harry seemed to have a habit of making a statement into a question. A waitress was now holding the door of the private room for them.

In the middle was a big round table, illuminated by a huge chandelier hung from a low ceiling. Almost immediately, Margaret blinked a few times to shield her eyes from the bright light. Whether it was made of genuine crystal was no concern of hers. She just couldn't care for a decorative object that was so out of place. Before she had time to make other observations of the private room, Harry's parents and another woman in her thirties were walking towards them.

Margaret greeted them in one of the few phrases she knew, "Nihao." On hearing the perfect pronunciation, the younger woman held Margaret's hands in hers and started speaking in Putonghua. Margaret smiled and nodded, even though she could not make head or tail of what she said.

"Leave her alone, Mengying," said Harry. "Margaret doesn't speak Putonghua."

"She does. She said 'nihao,' and she smiles at my joke," said Mengying.

"Margaret was only trying to be polite." Harry turned to Margaret and said, "Don't mind Mengying. She is my elder cousin."

"Hello, Mengying, nice to meet you."

Margaret's second greeting in English brought a shy smile on her face. Like Harry and his friend, Ma Qiang, Mengying wouldn't stop staring at her new foreign friend.

As Margaret was speaking to Harry and his cousin, their parents were exchanging greetings with one another. Standing by the door, Ma Qiang was talking to some waitress, seemingly arranging drinks for everyone.

When greetings and introductions were done, Mr. Chen announced, "All right, let us get seated for lunch." He led the way by walking to the seat directly facing the door and said, "Come, Mr. and Mrs. Young, come and sit beside me."

Mr. Chen directed Margaret's parents to sit on his left side, placing Margaret's father next to him. Mrs. Chen clearly knew the rule and let the couple sit together. She sat next to Margaret's mother as soon as her guests took their seats.

"Harry, I'll leave it for you to look after the young people," said Mr. Chen.

It was too late for Margaret to choose her own seat; Harry was already guiding her to the other side of the table. Under his direction, she was made to sit next to him and Mengying. She knew it would be an interesting lunch with Putonghua streaming into her right ear and English on the left. When she saw an empty seat between Harry and his father, she naturally asked if they should move up one seat.

"We are expecting more guests," said Harry. "That will be for General Li. He always sits next to Father. They have a lot to talk about—business, international affairs, politics, and so on."

"Don't bore our guests with your nonsense, Harry. Help them with drinks and talk later," said Mr. Chen in his firm and commanding voice.

Whoever this General Li was, he wasn't the next person to arrive. As the waitress was serving tea, a family entered the room.

"Lou Ma, welcome," greeted Mr. Chen. "Let me introduce our friends from Canada to you." Mr. Ma came over to shake hands with everyone.

Margaret didn't understand why this young-looking Mr. Ma was addressed as *Lou*. He didn't look old at all.

"Look at Xiao Xiangxiang! She is such a big girl now. Come over here and sit on Uncle's lap," said Mr. Chen.

The girl appeared to be not much older than four. She first looked at her mother, waiting for a signal of consent before walking over to Mr. Chen. He welcomed her with open arms, sat her on his lap, and gave her his full attention. The little girl was extremely well-behaved and hardly moved on Mr. Chen's lap, like his little pet.

"Xiangxiang always smells nice, like a little flower," said Mr. Chen. Then, someone put a glass of orange juice in front of her. "It's for you. Drink it."

As Xiangxiang was happily drinking her juice from a straw, Mr. Chen lovingly stroked her face. She reminded Margaret of the little girl who sang at the opening ceremony of the Beijing Olympic Games. She wondered if all little girls in China were so well-behaved.

"Isn't she sweet?" said Harry. "My father adores Xiangxiang. Every time he sees her, he urges me to get married." He then exchanged a meaningful look with his cousin before putting his hand on Margaret's shoulder. Mengying nodded and smiled at Margaret in a way to put more weight to Harry's words. They were acting as though conspiring to set her up. What did they want from her? This was only her third encounter with this man, and her first meal with him. Margaret wondered if marriages were so speedily arranged in China.

Stealing a glance at Harry, Margaret had to admit that he was actually quite handsome. Other than his bad hairstyle, he had no major flaws. Unlike men in Hong Kong, Harry had a typical look of the northerners, meaning that he was tall and well-built with broad shoulders. His eyes, though not very big, were sharp and would stare at someone as though they could peer into your mind and heart. He would be any Chinese woman's dream date, but definitely not for Margaret, although she couldn't quite put her finger on the reason. Would it be that his hands that were not well manicured, or the fact that every time he pronounced words such as *think*, he made them sound like *sink*? Would these small details matter to a relationship? Margaret wondered. Would they matter more to her now than when she was younger? She had very little experience with Chinese men. From what she could remember of Nathan, it was possible that he also had some major flaws that she did not notice before. But why on earth was she thinking of Nathan now? Was it because he was the only Chinese man she had ever dated?

Margaret had no time to ponder over these issues, for she had to see what the commotion was about. Xiangxiang suddenly became too heavy for Mr. Chen and was ordered to get off of his lap. Under Harry's instructions, the Ma family was now seated. Mrs. Ma was put next to Mrs. Chen so the two women could catch up with each other. Beside Mrs. Ma was her daughter, Xiangxiang, who sat between her parents. Ma Luk took a seat furthest away from but directly opposite to the host. This seating arrangement was by no means arbitrary or casual. Margaret began to understand that the host had put a lot of thought into it. It was as though Mr. Chen was playing a game of chess, placing his pieces in strategic positions.

Upon receiving a signal from Mr. Chen, Ma Qiang instructed the head waitress to deliver drinks. All the men were given baijiu, a Chinese white liquor. Unlike the three Chinese women who drank tea, Margaret and her mother had a beer each. They might disagree on pretty much everything, but when it came to drinks with a Chinese meal, they always chose the same without fail. After the drinks came a few small dishes of appetizers.

"Let's eat," said Mr. Chen.

"Shall we wait for General Li?" asked Margaret's father.

"No, it's not necessary to wait for him," said Mr. Chen. "He usually gets stuck in some sort of meeting. When he finally shows up, he would usually have eaten. He only joins us for drinks."

After the appetizers there were more dishes, one of which was, of course, the long-awaited famous Peking duck, a speciality that was served in all important meals. A piece of succulent meat wrapped with cucumber and spring onion was a rather harmless way to seduce any business partner into making an agreement. Would Margaret be lured into something that she wasn't quite prepared for?

At the beginning of the meal, they only had a round of drinks before each course of food, but later on, drinking became more and more frequent, with or without the arrival of a new dish. Margaret and her mother were spared this wild frenzy of drinking in pairs. Two people were singled out each time so they would take it in turns to drink to one another, sometimes with a reason, but more often with none. Slowly and gradually, they didn't even bother to create one.

"Mr. Young and Lou Ma, why don't the two of you drink for a round?" said Harry's father. "Lou Ma is in charge of the restaurant licencing issues. You can't open a restaurant in Beijing without getting his approval."

"That's not true," said Ma Luk. "I'm just one of the officials."

"But you are the top one," said Mr. Chen. "Well, nearly. All you need is one more promotion, which I am sure you will get next year."

"Let me propose a toast then," said Margaret's father. "Let us wish Mr. Ma the best of luck for his promotion." Everyone, including Xiangxiang, now stood up and raised their glass.

"Wait. Am I missing a big celebration?" a new voice asked.

Entering the room was a man of six foot three. Every step made a thud on the carpet, so there was no mistake of his military bearing. Other than being very tall and well-built, he stood out differently from Harry and Ma Qiang, probably because of his hairstyle. Unlike the two young men who put gel on their hair, this man had a clean crew cut. Definitely more natural. Margaret wondered what made these men look so different from each other. Would it be Harry's overseas education or General Li's military training that set them apart?

"Come, General Li," greeted Mr. Chen. "We were about to drink to Lou Ma—A pre-celebration of his promotion."

"Oh, yes, the promotion. It's just a matter of time," said General Li.

As everyone was still having their glass raised in the air, waiting for General Li to join them, Margaret asked in a lowered voice, "Why is he so sure of Mr. Ma's promotion?"

"Oh, he knows everything. He attends all the important meetings," said Harry.

"Now, Xiangxiang, come over here. You must drink to your father's success." In one arm, General Li lifted the little girl into the air and let her sit on his forearm. He raised a glass in the other hand. After a round of drinks, General Li continued to fill the glasses for everyone.

Watching Xiangxiang go back to her seat and drink orange juice by herself, General Li suddenly felt sorry for her, and said, "Poor Xiangxiang has no one to play with. She's always on her own, listening to our boring conversations. Lou Ma, it's time to give her a little brother. Lou Chen, what do you think?"

"I couldn't agree more," responded Harry's father.

It was as if General Li had made an important decision for his friend; his suggestion prompted another round of drinks.

Recognising a few words in Putonghua, Margaret asked, "I thought families are allowed only one child in China. Isn't that so?"

"There's always a way to get round this policy," said Harry as he was stealing a look at Mengying from the corner of his eye. He then smiled at both ladies sitting close to him.

It was a quick glance, but Margaret saw it and registered its meaning. In disguise under a different relationship, this elder cousin could possibly be an illegitimate sister. No wonder she made every effort to ensure Margaret's comfort and well-being.

When the meal was finished, the sun had already set, and Margaret's father was so drunk that he had to be carried back to the hotel. How the other men who drank as much, if not more than her father managed not to show any physical sign of drunkenness was beyond her comprehension.

Did Margaret enjoy the meal? Part of it. She had tried the special Peking duck, which was claimed to be even better than that served at state dinners. Also, she had witnessed a well-behaved girl who would obey everyone without causing any trouble. Was the Peking duck a good enough reason to lure her into a deal, be it a business or a personal one? Most likely not. Margaret was not yet prepared to adopt a Chinese way of doing business. Perhaps she never would. Getting her father so drunk was the last straw. Margaret had imagined many different possibilities for her future, but none of them came close to dying with a failed liver. She would rather stick with her small company.

PART VI
1st OCTOBER, 2014
HONG KONG

OUR MOVEMENT

It was Kate's idea of "being there" to experience the event. "Watching it on TV doesn't count. It means nothing, nothing at all," she insisted. "Besides, it's not just an event; it's ours. Something big is at last happening in our city."

Kate had her own theory of making sense of the political changes that Hong Kong underwent over the past seventeen years since the handover of its sovereignty to China. Neither a politician nor someone interested in politics, Kate did not usually pay too much attention to what the government was doing. She was merely an ordinary citizen who would rather spend her time shopping, travelling, and trying out exotic food. But the Umbrella Movement hit close to home. When it escalated, she felt acute concern at its development. Out of self-interest, she was eager to find out how the event would affect her livelihood in the immediate and, more importantly, the distant future. Although nobody could put a safe bet on their future, Kate figured that hard-working people like her deserved better security. It wouldn't be fair to work her whole life, saving up for a pension that would only be snatched away in her old age, leaving her with nothing but a jaw-dropping moment. Kate really disliked unethical policy or irresponsible leadership, and least of all police brutality. When tear gas was used on the night of the twenty-eighth, she was furious.

"Did you see what happened? Did you see that on TV?" Margaret remembered Kate's opening line as soon as she picked up her phone. "I couldn't believe my eyes! How could the police use such violence on the young people?"

"I know it's bad, but what do you expect?" said Margaret. "I had this feeling that it was a matter of time before the police got tough. And I was right. Don't you see? The government must be desperate, as National Day is drawing close. They want to clean up the city, so everything will be back to normal. Don't you think so?"

"What's wrong with you? You are taking everything as a matter of course." Kate let her voice show a slight irritation.

"What do you think then?" asked Margaret.

"I think it's the end of Hong Kong; it's the end of the one-country, two-system policy," said Kate.

"You sound like my mom."

"Did your mother make the same comment?"

"She did, but not this time. She made a similar comment many years ago when she was watching the tanks moving into Tiananmen Square on TV. Now that she lives in Canada, she doesn't really care about what happens here. She doesn't follow the news in Hong Kong anymore."

"See? Nothing's changed, history repeats itself," said Kate.

"Perhaps you are right. But we can't do anything, can we?"

"I'll keep watching the news to find out how things will develop. You know, I have my future to think of. Besides, I want to witness history first-hand," said Kate. "Twenty-five years ago, I only watched it on TV like your mother, but not this time. I'll tell you what, I will check with my brother and his friends. As soon as I know what they are up to, I'll give you a call. Okay?"

"What makes you think I will go along with your plan?" asked Margaret.

"Of course you will," said Kate. "You are one of us."

"I am so honoured to be treated as a local; thank you," said Margaret.

The tear gas tactic, which was meant to scare people away and drive them home, ended up rather unexpectedly, adding impetus for more to join in on the first of October, the National Day of the People's Republic of China. Having seen images of young people with their simple protective gear, namely goggles and umbrellas, people couldn't help feeling sorry for them. These were young people who thought their brave act could change the system and make the place fairer and happier for everyone. It was their belief and conviction that melted the hearts of even those who were lazy and complacent.

The government had to be caught by surprise by the scale of the movement and its publicity among the foreign media. With a wrong move, there might be a repeat of the Tiananmen Square incident. Same as what happened in the capital city in 1989, the Umbrella Movement started with people's dissatisfaction with their livelihoods. As frustration intensified, students joined in and reacted with class boycotts and mass gatherings. The main difference between this and the event that took place in Beijing was that, other than the presence of foreign press, modern technology allowed anyone with a smart phone to make a video go viral within seconds. With the great amount of public attention, Margaret knew that the government wouldn't dare to make any stupid decisions on National Day. This would give her a perfect opportunity to witness the movement first-hand, her first encounter with local politics, in the company of Kate and her brother.

What Margaret did not tell Kate on the phone was how she got mixed up in another students' movement twenty-five years ago. She figured that since she had not told anyone about this before, there was no reason why she should bring up the matter now. Besides, she wasn't even sure of the identity of this friend of Dominic's. Was he really a student activist? Yang could be his first or his last name. An image of someone wearing a monochrome T-shirt was all she could remember. Their encounter was brief, and it left no traces on Margaret's life path. And yet what was happening in Hong Kong at the moment triggered her memory of the past, and it saddened her. Why? Probably because these young people reminded her of Dominic. She felt sorry that, other than cutting his own life short, his suicide stirred no ripples to the movements, then and now.

Dragging herself out of bed, Margaret regretted not having turned down Kate's request to meet in the morning. After working for a month to secure a lucrative contract with the help of her staff, she desperately wanted to catch up on her sleep.

Thinking back to what Kate said the night before, she couldn't help feeling dubious about their arrangement.

"Let us meet at ten. How about Admiralty? What is it? Did you say too early? Okay, why don't you come later? You have your beauty sleep. As soon as I meet up with the others, I will come and get you at the station . . . What time? I don't know. I have no idea what the plan will be. Call me when you arrive, okay?"

What sort of plan was that? Meeting at the Admiralty Station at a time unspecified was something new to Margaret. But she didn't want to argue with her best friend. *If I arrive a little after ten, I might be able to catch her there,* Margaret thought with a sigh.

The moment she arrived at the station, she gave her friend a buzz. "I'm here at the Admiralty Station. Where are you?"

"Why didn't you call me first? We are now in MK," said Kate.

"Oh, shall I come over to meet you there?" asked Margaret.

"No, you'd better not," said Kate.

"I thought we are meeting at Admiralty."

"That was what I suggested last night, but things have changed quickly. Anyway, you'd better stay where you are. It's much more organised on your side than here. People in Admiralty are better behaved, more civilised, if you see what I mean. I'll call you later."

"Where are you? Can I come and join you?" Kate hung up before Margaret could finish her question. She was about to call again, for she wanted to castigate her friend for messing up her holiday, but then she thought better of it. No matter how much she disliked being left out the last minute, she knew Kate had her reason. *I'll just have a quick walk around and then go home and enjoy a quiet afternoon on my own.* Margaret decided that it would be a much better way of spending her day off.

So, on she walked along Rodney Road before turning left into Queensway, which was a wide boulevard with eight lanes, including the middle tram tracks running in opposite directions, the east and the west. Margaret heard on the news that this road was closed for traffic because of the mass gathering. Now walking along it, she had an eerie feeling. The city that was always packed with people was suddenly abandoned by both citizens and those who ruled them.

Where are the students? Margaret wondered. She walked for more than a minute without coming across a single soul. Other than leaves rustling in the light breeze and birds chirping along, she heard almost nothing. For some reason, Margaret really enjoyed this moment of solitude. How strange it would be but yet how content might she be to live in a city alone? It was really weird to see bus stops with no one waiting. Margaret almost mistook the life-size female models displayed in advertisements for real.

As she walked further along towards Wanchai, Margaret began to see people clustering in small groups, taking photos or strolling along a tram track without a single vehicle. They didn't look like student activists but were perhaps onlookers like herself. She asked a couple standing next to her, "Do you know where the mass gathering is taking place?"

Hearing her perfect Cantonese, they first looked her up and down before the woman pointed at the direction of Harcourt Road. Neither of them said a word. What were they thinking of? Couldn't they tell she was one of them? In a moment like now, Margaret wished Kate were here with her.

As she was climbing the steps of the footbridge that allowed pedestrians to cross the eight-lane highway, she slowed down her pace. On the wall of the stairwell were hundreds of stick-it notes with writings mostly in Chinese characters and some with nicely drawn cartoons. Even with her limited reading comprehension, Margaret could somehow decipher the codes and translate them into people's voices and their chanting in her head. She could sense the frustration of all these writers who had to be mostly young people, pleading a fair and open government—in other words, a better tomorrow.

Margaret was greatly moved and had a lot of sympathy for these young people who probably were not aware that their notes wouldn't stay for long. Very soon, the municipal workers would come and clean up everything. When the crowds dispersed, most people would carry on with their lives as though nothing had happened. There might be talk in the beginning. *It was a nuisance, but only a very small one,* they would say. Most people would repeat these words until voices of the indifferent majority drowned out those of the protesters. Margaret recalled how frustrated Dominic was on seeing his friends' inaction. Would people get more involved this time? Or would they still think that they could get by by kowtowing to those in power?

Margaret had no answers to any of these questions. All she knew was nothing lasted in Hong Kong. Trends came and went like a tide, but nothing lasted for long. But perhaps her perception was very different from that of the young protesters who wanted to preserve their way of life. Most of them were born in the 1990s when both the British and the Chinese governments were fully occupied with the handover. It was in this vacuum then a new local culture emerged. These young people were born at a time when there was no presence of a strong government. The British influence was gradually diminishing, and yet the Chinese government did not manage to extend its iron fist in time. This honeymoon period allowed people to form an illusion that they could truly be their own masters. What a romantic view! Though she did not completely share the same sentiments, Margaret secretly hoped that these young people were right.

Now, standing at the top of the footbridge, her eyes were met with hundreds, or even thousands, of people sitting on the asphalted road. Very different from images shown on mainstream TV channels, they did nothing destructive. Clustered in groups talking, reading, or sharing snacks, they formed an orderly and harmless mass. Kate was right to call them civilised, but to Margaret, they seemed absurdly amateurish. How could she not wish them luck when these young protesters were so disciplined that they would even recycle their rubbish?

It was surely a world event. Foreign journalists walked hurriedly up and down along the footbridge that was shared by everyone including filming crews from major broadcasting companies. Margaret was completely drawn to this atmosphere of youth and vitality. A man was painting on his easel, capturing an image of the mass gathering below. Four or five people who had no apparent connections with one another were each holding a placard that displayed their individual concerns. One of them jokingly wrote in support of a local actor to be elected as the next Chief Executive of Hong Kong.

Kate's change of plan in the last minute turned out to be the best arrangement or Margaret wouldn't have witnessed this event which would definitely go down in history. Walking along the footbridge, she treasured every single moment. She turned her head left and right, trying to take in as much as she could.

A CHANCE ENCOUNTER

Margaret kept walking and saw that everyone had a role to play. Everyone was busy doing something. From time to time, she came across volunteers who gave out bottled water for free. If she had been with Kate and her gang, she would have been doing something useful too, but for now she was merely an onlooker, someone who made no contributions but only increased human traffic, creating chaos and confusion to this otherwise peaceful demonstration. Suddenly, a bunch of people shoved their way rudely through the crowd. Margaret lost her balance and nearly fell onto the floor had she not been steadied by someone standing close to her.

"Thank you," said Margaret in English.

"You are welcome. Are you okay?" asked the man who was still holding her elbow so she wouldn't be further pushed by other passersby.

As Margaret was thanking the man and cursing under her breath those who pushed her, she gave a quick glance at her saviour. What a question! How could she be all right when the face she had been longing to touch finally materialised in front of her? She had to appear as shocked as the man. This chance encounter caught them both by surprise. They did not know what to say or how to act. Unlike film actors who acted out a scene a number of times to get it right, Margaret and Nathan had no script to follow. In close proximity, they simply looked at one another, studying a face that was once dearly loved.

It was impossible to stay put in crowded places. They were being pushed again, this time so hard that their faces almost touched.

"We'd better get out of here," said Nathan.

"Ouch," cried Margaret.

"What's wrong?"

"I think I've sprained my ankle."

"Is it painful? Can you walk?" asked Nathan.

Margaret took great care in taking a step with her good foot and tapping small steps with the toes of her injured one. "If you can walk me to the taxi stand, I shall be okay."

"Please let me check it. I'll take you to a clinic, if necessary," said Nathan.

"I'll be fine."

"I won't let you go unless I know you are absolutely fine. Remember? I was a professional athlete. I can tell how bad your injury is if you let me check it," insisted Nathan.

With Nathan's help, Margaret managed to hobble to an area that was less crowded. This was an intersection that connected the footbridge to a block of office buildings and a five-star hotel. As soon as they found an empty bench to rest, Margaret slipped off her shoes. She had no time to consider whether she should accept or reject help, for Nathan was already kneeling in front of her, checking her ankle.

"It has swollen a bit, otherwise it is no big deal," said Nathan as he was gently massaging Margaret's ankle. "I have some ointment in my hotel room. Come, let me help you." Nathan assisted Margaret to stand up and steadied her with his arms round her waist.

"Are you staying in this hotel?"

"Yes. You see, I don't live in Hong Kong anymore. I only come back for a holiday." Nathan corrected himself after a short pause, "Actually for business this time."

As she was struggling with what to do, she felt a pain shooting up the nerves upon a slight touch. "Ouch, it really hurts."

"See, it's not a good idea to put any pressure on it," said Nathan. "But if you let it rest for a few hours, you will be able to walk again."

A few hours? That would give her plenty of time to find out about him and Tsz Ching. What Alan had told her was probably rumour or his imagination. They might not be together anymore. Did he say he no longer lived in Hong Kong? Would he be living in China now?

Limping into Nathan's spacious room with an en-suite bathroom, Margaret was glad that she did not insist on going home on her own. She sank into a single armchair and let Nathan give her delayed first aid. He was indeed experienced with injuries. It wasn't long before the pain gradually decreased. When her ankle was professionally bandaged, the swelling was temporarily out of sight.

"Thank you," said Margaret. "I'd better leave now."

"Wait, put your foot up." Nathan put a chair in front of Margaret. "If you leave now, you will hurt yourself again."

"But I can't just stay in your room. You surely must have made some other plans."

"As a matter of fact, I haven't. My only plan was to go and see what those young people are up to. Now that I've seen it, I really have too much time on my hands." Met with no response, he continued, "Besides, I really want to catch up with you."

Margaret looked at him curiously, wondering if he meant what he said.

"How about eating lunch together? I can order room service."

The suggestion reminded her that she had left home without any breakfast. Almost immediately, she heard her stomach rumbling, and she gave an embarrassed laugh. It wasn't long before they laughed together, like old times.

As Nathan was ordering their meal over the phone, Margaret made a mental note of the things that involved a human touch. Two beds were made, both single, and not a sign of disorder. It was difficult to tell the number of occupants at a glance. She moved her eyes to the side tables for more tell-tale signs. On one of them lay three watches, all of them men's. The room was neat and tidy, not even a suitcase was in sight. Other than the watches, the only personal item was a pack of documents and a laptop on the writing desk. Margaret was almost certain that Nathan was the only person using the room. It was a relief, for she didn't want to bump into Tsz Ching. That would be unnecessarily embarrassing.

As her searching eyes met with Nathan's, Margaret commented casually, "You keep your room in good order."

"Oh, yes. My boss has the habit of inviting himself into my room anytime he chooses. And he can never stand a messy room. The person who held my position before got fired just because of that."

"Chinese?" asked Margaret.

"Do you mean my boss or the person before me? No, my boss is German, but yes, if you mean the unlucky person. Poor guy, none of his credits were mentioned in his appraisal. He was only referred to as a highly disorganised person. He actually did a lot for the company. A few years ago, when our company started expanding into the Chinese market, this person did a lot of groundwork to make that happen. When I joined the company last year, it was running quite smoothly."

"Will it be all right if your boss finds me here?"

"Don't worry, he didn't join me on this business trip. What I meant was that his habit has become mine. Like him, I feel compelled to keep things in order. It has become my second nature." After a short pause, he added apologetically, "I must be boring you. I don't know what happened to me. I can't find the right words to express myself. Perhaps seeing you again makes me feel," he paused briefly, "a little giddy."

Before he got too emotional, Margaret changed the subject tactfully, "Are you still in the fashion industry?"

"No, not anymore. My company deals with all kinds of machines, basically anything that makes money. By the way, how did you know I was in fashion?"

Margaret ignored Nathan's question. Instead, she continued to probe for more information. "I didn't know you were into engineering."

"Me? Into engineering? Of course not. I am what you call a middleman. Not even my boss is an engineer, but he certainly understands machines better than I do. My boss and I are in charge of negotiating and closing business deals. We have a team to follow up on the technical issues."

Margaret was hoping to find out more about Nathan while she was waiting for her foot to heal, but she did not want to appear too direct or too pushy. For now, it was so much safer and less embarrassing to talk about someone she hadn't met before. She continued to play the role as the inquisitor. "How about the person who got fired? Was he an engineer?"

"Oh, no. He knew nothing about engineering. He was employed for a different reason. He had a lot of useful contacts in China, if you see what I mean."

Margaret saw exactly what Nathan meant and still remembered the time when her parents tried to pull a few strings to open the China market for her business. Whether the people she met had great power or not, she didn't care anymore. Margaret was happy not to have taken up that path, or she wouldn't be running her business according to her own wishes.

"What about you? Do you have a lot of contacts?" asked Margaret.

"Not in the beginning, but I'm getting better now. What happened was that he and I worked alongside for a while. In those few months, he introduced all the important people to me, of course without knowing that he would be made redundant soon. I still remember how he talked about his ideas for new projects. Poor guy!"

Calling him a "poor guy" for a second time, Nathan somehow showed such empathy in his words that one might be mistaken about his good intentions. How would anyone have guessed that he later took the job from his predecessor and that he did so without any guilty feelings? A victorious smile on his face, no matter how faint it was, caught Margaret's attention and caused her a moment of unease. The only way to confirm whether it was only her imagination was to focus her next series of questions on Nathan. Unexpectedly, a harmless question led to an emotional outburst.

"So, how long will you be in Hong Kong?" asked Margaret.

"Not long, maybe a week or so, depending on the progress of work."

"Oh, I see," said Margaret with an emphasis on the first word.

"Are you disappointed? Nobody seems to care how long I stay in town anymore, not since my mother passed away. My sister is so busy with her kids that I don't always get to see her."

"I am sorry to hear about your mother."

"That's all right. She died of old age. How about your parents? How are they? I remember your father a lot. He's such a nice man. I remember how he encouraged me to be the best swimmer in Hong Kong."

"Really? When did he say that to you?"

"Oh, you know, when I saw you off at the airport. That was the only time we met."

That was, in fact, the last time Margaret and Nathan saw one another. Suddenly, in her mind's eye, the goodbye scene flashed back: friends and relatives taking photos with her, Nathan hugging her, saying goodbye to Cindy, taking a box of egg tarts from Tsz Ching. Nathan might be recalling the same scene in his own way. For a long while, they remained silent, catching up with their lost time, until a knock came at the door.

"It must be our room service." Nathan broke the silence and went to answer the door.

Margaret excused herself into the bathroom while Nathan directed the housekeeper to set the table for lunch.

"What am I doing here?" Her reflection in the mirror gave no reply. In the tight space, Margaret struggled whether she should embrace this reunion or reject it. She wondered if this chance encounter would be one of her so-called turning points in life. For no reason at all, an image popped up in her mind: Nathan was sitting on a sofa with her, holding her hands as they were watching TV together. She wasn't sure if it was a memory from the past or a projection of the future. A picture of domestic life that flashed across her mind nevertheless gave her courage to continue with this adventure, convincing herself that it was a good sign. She quickly freshened up before reappearing at her best.

The sight and smell of prawn dumplings and freshly fried spring rolls were irresistibly appetising.

"Good choice. I like dim sum." Margaret couldn't help showing a satisfied smile.

"How could I forget what you like!" exclaimed Nathan as he was navigating on his computer. "Let me put some music on, and then I'll come and open the champagne."

"What are we celebrating?" asked Margaret.

"It is National Day, isn't it?"

"Oh! That."

"Shouldn't we be glad to have a day off? Or else we wouldn't have had the chance to wander in the street and bump into one another."

"Yes, literally," said Margaret.

"Yes, literally," repeated Nathan idiotically.

"But I don't usually drink in the daytime." It was one of her resolutions, made a long while ago after she witnessed how drunk her father was at the Peking duck banquet.

"Easy. I have a way to change the time. I'll make sure you don't feel guilty." Nathan went to the windows to close all the curtains. In a short time, the atmosphere completely changed. The reading lamp by the bedside and the light in the entrance hall gave a soft halo to every object, including Nathan. Having adjusted to the dim lighting, Margaret could now see Nathan walking back to the table, holding a bottle of champagne and an ice bucket in each hand. Popping the cork, he poured a glass for each, and said, "Let's remember today. Cheers."

Their glasses clinked before Nathan sat down and started serving food on their plates. It was at that moment when Nathan started explaining his years of absence.

"I am sorry that I stopped calling you. You might think that I tried to avoid you. To tell you the truth, I was scared. You won't believe it, but I really had a hard life. People only see how well we perform in sport and forget what life is like for an athlete. We are under the spotlight only for a few minutes.

What happens after that? Out of sight, out of mind. Those long hours of practice, so harsh and so repetitive, not to mention the injuries, and the pain. Yes, I had to deal with pain, a lot of it, in my mind and in my body. There were times I couldn't convince myself continuing. If I took a regular job, I should at least have my days off, but being a professional athlete, I didn't have any rest."

"You had the glory," reminded Margaret.

"Oh, yes, the glory. I won many prizes. I had such a big collection of trophies too. But they were nothing; they didn't fatten me up, and they certainly didn't make me rich."

"I thought you like winning."

"Yes, I did, and I still do. I think anyone who plays sports professionally enjoys winning, which is why I felt so much pressure. Every day, I had that constant fear of losing my championship. I suppose I had no time to think about others but myself. I had to be a very selfish person then."

Margaret mistook his pause and thought that he was going to say how sorry he was for not visiting her in Canada. Instead, he said in a slightly raised voice, "How about you? What have you been doing all these years? When did you come back to Hong Kong?"

"I came back in 2004, so nearly ten years now. I am running a small business. I reckon that it's a lot easier to work for myself than for other people." Margaret decided to skip the part about her failed marriage.

"What sort of business is it?"

"A consultancy firm specialising in fine dining. I mainly help overseas clients set up their business here in Hong Kong."

"I didn't know you are an expert on food, or I would have ordered something different. Maybe French cuisine or something posh. By the way, why Hong Kong only? China is such a big market. If you knew how much people in Shanghai and Beijing are spending in restaurants just for one night, you wouldn't be happy with just the Hong Kong market. I know many government officials in Beijing. They can make things happen for you once they treat you as their friend."

"I know." Margaret remembered her trip to Beijing with her parents and friends.

"You do?" Nathan said with his eyebrow raised. "Perfect. I don't need to talk you into it. I can guarantee your business will be bigger and more profitable."

"You seem to be speaking from your own experience."

"Definitely. For me to switch from a sportsman to a businessman, it requires more than just hard work and skills. It's my luck. I was lucky to have attended the Beijing Olympics."

"Me too, I attended the opening ceremony," said Margaret.

"Oh, really? It's amazing that we were both there. If only we had met then . . ." Nathan paused for a while to collect his thoughts. "Did you watch the swimming competitions? They were so exciting, and of course I knew all the swimmers."

Margaret didn't want to tell Nathan that she only attended the opening ceremony and did not watch a single game. So, she directed the course of their conversation by prompting him to elaborate on his luck.

"Oh, that's because I met so many important people in the event, or I wouldn't have made several lucrative deals for my company."

"The German company?"

"No, I was still working for a fashion company called Flamingo. Have you heard of it?"

"Yes, of course. I like fashion."

"I can tell. Anyway, that was a life-changing moment for me. For many years, I'd been trying to downplay my weakness."

"I can't imagine you have any."

If there was a hint of irony in Margaret's words, Nathan did not notice. He responded as if he were attending an interview. "That I did not attend university. But of course, I don't think about it anymore. There was a time I considered it a stumbling block in my career, but actually it wasn't. In a way, I'm glad that I didn't study in the university, or I wouldn't be so flexible with the choice of my job. I am happy to be a merchandiser, a shop manager, or an entrepreneur. I can be anything. Isn't that wonderful? I'm happy to work anywhere, as long as it pays."

Nathan suddenly became alive with cheering his lack of a degree.

For no apparent reason, Dominic's name flashed across Margaret's mind. Probably because both he and Nathan had to accept what life without a university qualification could offer. Would Dominic have also been working in China if he had not committed suicide?

"So, you are happy working in China now?"

"Yeah, but let's not talk about work. How about some more to drink for you?"

"Haven't we finished the bottle?"

"Only the first one." Nathan walked over to the small fridge. When he walked back to the table, he had a new bottle in his hand. "I'm always well-prepared when it comes to food and drink."

As he was pouring another glass for Margaret and himself, some classical music started flowing softly in the air, creating a truly romantic feeling. The food and champagne did wonders. Margaret forgot about the pain in her foot. She had indeed forgotten about everything: where she was and what brought them together again. She would be pleased for the moment to last for as long as it could. Then the music stopped. Whether there was any music did not matter, for the notes, like their memories, were still lingering in the air. In a state of euphoria, one longing look or simply a curve of lips was all it needed to reignite their love flame.

Margaret's eyes moved from Nathan's boyish grin to her hand that was slowly held in his. Suddenly, time and space had no existence. In a close encounter, two bodies were reaching out to one another, yearning for their lost youth. Margaret could still taste champagne in her mouth, or was it at the tip of Nathan's? When the weight of Nathan's body became too much for her, Margaret simply let go of herself and lay flat on the neatly made bed. With eyes half shut, she didn't see much, and she did not want to. All she cared for at that moment was to feel Nathan's touch and her body's reaction to each of his strokes, first gentle, then getting more intense. His kissing and caressing did bring back fond memories. Margaret felt like a teenage girl again. She secretly hoped that it was a child's game. How she wished it to be a harmless game with no end!

The room as an entity of its own was, however, conscious of time. The silence that filled its space suddenly broke. For some reason, music resumed coming out from Nathan's laptop—Bach's piano pieces played in a jazzy style. This kind of music Margaret would very much love to hear over a drink in a bar, but in a love-making scene, it just didn't sound right. All the quick notes, rather than blending into a nice flow, gave a disjointed mood. The music was light-hearted but not seriously romantic, which was exactly how Margaret felt. When she saw how eager Nathan was at trying to excite them both, she found him laughable. Wasn't he trying to win her as much as he had wanted to win in a swimming competition? She couldn't help sniggering at his childish behaviour.

"What are you laughing at?" Nathan gave her a bewildered look.

"Nothing. I just think that it's a mistake."

"What mistake are you talking about?"

"I don't think I love you anymore." Margaret had no time to come up with a lie. In order not to hurt his ego, she said after a short pause, "Sorry."

"I am sorry too. We could have a lot of fun." Nathan quickly pulled up his pants and walked over to the table to get a drink.

"The thing is I have no desire for," Margaret wanted to say *you*, but instead she said, "this sort of fun."

"I understand what you mean." Holding a drink in his hand, Nathan continued to speak, but this time he did not offer Margaret a drink. "You are always a serious girl. You don't need a lot of fun, do you?"

"I don't see what you are trying to say."

Nathan sulked. "Do you not? This is the second time you've rejected me. You rejected me before, remember?"

"Stop acting like a child now. Didn't we have fun eating and drinking together?" said Margaret. "Besides, I haven't had such a good laugh in years. You know what? The pain is gone. I think I shall leave now."

What Margaret didn't tell Nathan was that she would reject him for a third, a fourth, and a fifth time if such a circumstance arose in the future. And why not? Another look at Nathan confirmed that she had made the right decision. Beyond his strong and shapely body, she saw absolutely nothing in this man. Maybe he didn't have a bad hairstyle, nor did he pronounce *think* as *sink* like Harry, but they were of the same kind. Margaret was pleased at not having gotten mixed up with them, or she would have been just *another* woman of theirs.

Nathan made a last attempt at keeping Margaret. "Do you really? Can we not see each other for a little longer? I might not come back to Hong Kong for a while."

"If I decide to expand my business into the market of China, I will call you."

"Will you? You must. Promise me."

"Let's see," said Margaret.

It was perhaps out of habit, or politeness, or a bit of both, that they exchanged their telephone numbers, even though Margaret knew that she would never contact him again. Unlike many years ago when they did the same on their first date, Margaret was no longer an inexperienced young woman. But all the same, she did as Nathan suggested. Of all the things that life had taught her, it was only right to end a relationship in style.

"I've been wanting to ask you something." She couldn't help clearing her mind once and for all.

"What is it?"

"You remember how you promised you would come and visit me in Winnipeg? Why didn't you?"

"I had no money, and my swimming team refused to sponsor me to compete in Canada. As simple as that," said Nathan.

"Really? I thought you had some other reason."

"No. What are you thinking of?"

"I don't know. Maybe you were attached to somebody?" asked Margaret.

"If you mean Tsz Ching, you are wrong. We were together for just a few months. Then I got so busy with my training that I had no time for anything else."

"But I heard a different story." After a short pause, Margaret added, "Anyway, Tsz Ching must love you a lot."

"Maybe, but our relationship wasn't deep. I don't know who's been telling you stories. The fact is, we were not together for a very long time."

"But soon after I left Hong Kong, right?" Margaret looked right into Nathan's eyes, seemingly reading his mind. With no hint of menace, she simply induced him to speak the truth with a gentle smile.

"All right, I'll tell you what you already knew then." Nathan took a deep breath and made his long overdue confession in one go.

"She started following me everywhere I went as soon as you left. She was super caring and very thoughtful of my needs. She took care of my training schedule and daily routine. Every time I lost a race or had a fight with you over the phone, she was always there for me, so it was natural that we finally went together, but it wasn't long before I realised it was a mistake. She's the jealous type. I tell you, I couldn't go anywhere without taking her with me. It would've been fine if she joined the group, but she refused to have anything to do with my friends. She only sat there by herself, with no facial expressions. Then I knew she only wanted to keep an eye on me.

"I felt suffocated and yelled at her so badly that she left. At first, I thought that was it. She would never forgive me calling her all those bad names. But after a month or so, she came back, promising me that she would change and would never try to manipulate me. The first two or three weeks was always peaceful, what you call a honeymoon period, but it didn't take long before she became her old self. So, I had no choice but to break up with her again. I forgot the number of break-ups we had. Even my friends got confused about our relationship. Anyone who didn't see me for a while would tease me by asking if I was *in love* or *out of love*. This went on for a year or two, until one day, maybe she felt that she had enough, or maybe she felt sorry for me, she left without saying goodbye." Nathan snapped his fingers. "Just like that, without a trace."

"Do you miss her? Did you go and look for her?" asked Margaret.

"No, why should I? In my mind, we had long separated."

Margaret gave a knowing smile.

"What is so funny to you?" said Nathan.

"Nothing." Margaret felt liberated. If Nathan could so easily shrug off his relationship with Tsz Ching, he would do the same to her. Margaret came to understand that she was not in love with this man anymore. Maybe she never was. What she experienced earlier was a softness that came with the music, but what had been in her hand gradually slipped through her fingers as if they were feathers, then water, until nothing else was there. If it had been an infatuation, it was a stubborn one that had refused to go away for years.

"Shall I take you home?" asked Nathan.

Margaret understood what he was hinting at and thought better of it. "No, I don't think so. I shall perhaps go home and lie down for a while. I must have spent too much time wandering in the crowds." Those were her parting words.

A LONG-DISTANCE CALL

Margaret was feeling exhausted when she arrived home and slept like a log for hours before her mobile phone rang.

She picked it up unwillingly. "Hello, who is it?"

"Are you already sleeping? What time is it?"

On hearing an accusing tone, Margaret sat up in her bed. "Mom?"

"Where have you been all day? I've been calling you."

"I was out. It's a public holiday in Hong Kong"

"I know. I saw it in the news."

"What did you see in the news? I thought you don't watch news about Hong Kong anymore?"

"Of course I do. I've been keeping an eye on the protests. What else?"

"Oh, you saw that? I thought you were not concerned."

"With you living alone in Hong Kong, how can I not be concerned?"

"What's up, Mom?"

"Are you busy?"

"No, it's not that. I just need some food. I'm starving now." Margaret hinted that she wasn't in a mood for chit-chat. "Let me eat first. I'll call you back, okay?"

Before Margaret finished what she had to say, her mother interrupted her, "Listen. Snowy died. I'm very sad, and I couldn't go to sleep."

"What did you say? Who died?"

"Snowy, I mean Bei-bei . . ." Her mother said no more, for she started crying.

Margaret waited patiently, recalling the early days of Bei-bei's puppyhood. How could she have forgotten to call her mother? She knew Bei-bei was diagnosed with a chronic renal problem two months ago, and her mother had to give her fluid therapy at home. It was a tough job, for her mother hated the sight of needles. Nevertheless, she forced herself to administer this medical measure for her beloved pet. Margaret also learned from her readings on a number of websites that animals reacted very differently to such treatment, largely dependent on their age. Bei-bei was old, so she didn't expect her to live much longer, but even so, it was heartbreaking to receive the news. After all, she was in charge of Bei-bei's early training. Margaret still remembered how in her puppyhood the four-legged furry animal ran around the house with her, sharing both her joys and sorrows. Bei-bei was there with her when Dominic stayed as a visitor. She was also the first one in the family to *know* about her engagement with Brent.

When her mother finally had her emotions under control, she said more cheerfully, "You know what? Hard times trigger creativity."

"Who has been creative?" asked Margaret.

"I wrote a poem for Snowy. You know, in her final days, I stayed awake almost every night to make sure she was okay. One night, I was nursing her as usual. I stayed by her side and observed her for a long time. I saw her fighting the disease. She wasn't even aware that I was there with her. At that point, I realised there was nothing I could do. Dying is such a sad, solo act, isn't it? The therapy I gave her seemed to be more for me than for her. Do you know what I mean? I couldn't help relieve her pain. The therapy I gave her only made me feel less guilty. At the end of the day, she had to fight it herself."

"You sound very philosophical, Mom. So, you wrote a poem for her?"

"Yes, I did. Want to hear it?"

"Of course."

Over the phone came Betty's clear, crisp voice reading the poem. "Ahem . . . "*How I Wish it to be This Moment*," that's the title of the poem."

"I like it," said Margaret.

"Listen . . .

How I wish it to be this moment,
Breathing in, breathing out,
Breathing in, breathing out,
Sliding down, limbs giving away, pulling down the weight,
Putting down the pain, the burden, the last breath.
How I wish it to be this moment,
Turning left, turning right,
Shaking a little, shivering from pain,
Getting up, sliding down,
Gasping, standing up again.
How I wish it to be this moment,
Squatting, half-leaning,
Gasping again, looking down, down, down.
Breathing in, breathing out,
Breathing in, breathing out,
Breathing in, breathing out,
Until no more."

Then came a long silence before Margaret collected herself. "It's a wonderful poem, Mom. I was touched."

"Are you really?"

"Of course. To be honest with you, when you first mentioned the poem, I didn't think much of it, but as I was listening to you, I could see Bei-bei in my mind's eye and picture how she suffered in her last days. I wish I were there with you. Mom. You must keep the poem and let me read it again when I come and see you in Canada."

"When will that be?"

"I don't know, maybe in the summer."

"I don't mean coming to see me for a few weeks. When are you coming back for good?"

"I haven't thought of that as a possible option."

"Don't you think it's time? You know worse things will come after the tear gas."

"Oh, don't worry. I can look after myself. Besides, it's not as bad as that."

"I know you won't like what I'm going to say. You have such a soft spot for the city, but I'll tell you something. You won't believe the number of people moving here from Hong Kong in the last couple of years. Remember Mr. and Mrs. Chan who used to live next door to us? I saw them in Chinatown the other day. The whole family is living here now."

"Really, you still recognise them?"

"Margaret, please don't change the subject. I want you to listen to me for once. I think I know Hong Kong better than you do, although it sounds absurd. But I don't have a preconception like you. I keep an open mind when I talk to people who have just moved here. After piecing their stories together, I think I get a rather clear picture."

"What kind of picture is it?"

"I'm afraid it's a rather gloomy one. Years ago, when we moved back to Canada, Hong Kong experienced a brain drain. Do you remember that?"

"Yes, I do."

"It's not much different now, only this time you don't see the headlines in the newspapers, which makes the whole thing even more secretive and scary."

"Mom, you sound like Kate and her friends."

"If they also think so, they should consider leaving Hong Kong. Canada is a big country, and people have big hearts. We accept everyone." Margaret's mother finally revealed her true intention of making this phone call. "Margaret, you must listen to me. I'm not doing this for myself or for your dad. I want you to be happy."

"I am happy. I have my business and my friends here."

"But not for long—I mean your business. What hope is there for your small company? If you are not one of those mega-rich, you can't even survive. If you don't like the idea of expanding into the north, you might as well sell the goodwill before it's too late," advised her mother.

"I'll think about it."

"Don't think for too long."

Margaret did not forget what her mother had said to her. Of course, she wouldn't be constantly thinking about it, but every now and then, bits of the conversation popped up in her mind, giving her a more objective view from somebody living outside Hong Kong.

As for her encounter with Nathan, Margaret kept it to herself. She didn't even mention a word to Kate. What was the point if she decided that their relationship, or rather her long-term infatuation, was over? On this fateful day, Margaret nevertheless was sure of one thing—that she did have a soft spot. As a teenager, she had no answer for her father who wondered if her first love would melt his daughter's heart, but now her mother seemed to have hit the nail on the head.

PART VII
20–
A PLACE CALLED HOME

Never have relish in the faery power
Of unreflecting love; then on the shore
Of the wide world I stand alone, and think
Till love and fame to nothingness do sink.

—John Keats, "When I Have Fears
That I May Cease to Be"

PREMONITIONS

For all her life, Margaret considered herself a local. She spoke fluent Cantonese, ate local food, and had a lot of Hong Kong friends. The last thing she expected was to be treated as a foreigner in her birthplace. Nothing was worse than being rid of in a cold, nonchalant manner. And that was exactly what happened. When her landlord refused to renew the lease for her office, using all sorts of excuses, Margaret first got worried, then became suspicious of his motive. Why would she need to foot the bill of renovating a small office? Besides, Margaret didn't see the need for a grand makeover. She liked the layout of her office; it was bright with plenty of sunshine. She didn't find it necessary to change anything, but of course her landlord thought otherwise. He wanted to subdivide the office into even smaller units. Whether there would be natural light was none of his concern. Renting the space out to eight or more tenants as opposed to a single one would make a huge difference to his bank account. With the dollar sign dangling in front of him, he made unreasonable demands on Margaret—first, a renovation fee, then a big increase in the rent.

The day Margaret decided that she'd had enough nonsense from her landlord, she walked out of the negotiating room, thinking that she would be able to find a new office out of her naïve ignorance of the political and financial situation. She didn't manage to rent another office. To continue with her business in Hong Kong, she either had to expand it in a very aggressive manner so that she could afford the high rent or be prepared to lose all her savings until it folded. She decided she might as well collect the small revenue that she had made over the years before it was too late. Margaret once thought of contacting Nathan for help, but the idea of changing her business model or even losing control of her own direction really scared her. Or she could have followed the path like a few of her rivals by making questionable deals with businesspeople from China. As long as she didn't ask about the source of their funds, they would keep pumping money into her company. But could she do that with a clear conscience?

It was a tough decision. She couldn't imagine herself closing her business and leaving. What would happen to her staff? What would happen to her city? Margaret had a premonition that if she chose to leave Hong Kong for a second time, it would be for good. On nights when she lay sleepless in bed, she tried to convince herself that there was nothing wrong with a Chinese business model. She just had to learn it, and she was almost sure that Nathan would guide her. She only had to ask.

Margaret nearly made that phone call, had Kate's youngest brother and his friends not been arrested and jailed after the Umbrella Movement. At first, Margaret received the news with disbelief. Why were they not arrested during the movement but so many years later? If they had committed a crime, shouldn't they have been arrested there and then? Why did the government wait for years before it took action? When people were still trying to make sense of the movement, now they had to deal with the shock of all these arrests and imprisonments. Even when Kate's brother was sent to jail, Margaret still hoped that it was a mistake. All the government wanted to do was to teach these youngsters a lesson, she reasoned. A moment of awakening finally arrived when she learned that these activists would not be released for years.

The unfair sentences aside, what induced Margaret to leave Hong Kong was a personal tragedy. She got a very nasty case of food poisoning after eating a farewell meal with her staff. Somebody suggested a Sichuanese hot-pot dinner, and everyone cheered at the idea. She wanted to turn it down, for her taste buds were not meant for hot and spicy food. But then she figured that it would most likely be the last time she ate with everyone in her staff. She went along with their choice anyhow.

They ordered food of all kinds, pretty much every single item on the menu. Her staff volunteered to cook for her. She only had to watch them slide those meatballs, fish balls, and slices of beef by the side of the pot and turn them skilfully in the soup with a large spoon. The sight of food swimming in red, oily, bubbly liquid aroused Margaret's curiosity. As she drank her beer, she couldn't resist trying some seafood, which surprisingly didn't turn out to be very spicy. She only felt a tingling numbness on her tongue. Not a bad sensation. So, she continued eating and drinking while everyone took their turns cracking jokes and telling funny stories. Whenever the conversation started to falter, they kept eating and drinking in order that the party did not lose its momentum. Margaret kept reminding herself to go easy with the food, but even so, as a novice, the amount was enough to make her fall sick. She later found out that everyone in the party got food poisoning, only that it was a lot worse for her.

The moment she arrived home she had to rush to the toilet, throwing up. After half an hour of suppressing an urge to vomit and losing it, she was sick as a dog. Using her last ounce of energy, Margaret just managed to call for an ambulance. She then suffered in pain for a few more hours before the medical staff in the emergency ward attended to her. There was no use to ask, threaten, or beg, since her case was not life-threatening. When Margaret was not spending her time in the toilet, she struggled to find a spot in the waiting room where she could rest a little. *How come there are so many sick people in Hong Kong, and they all need medical help at midnight!* Margaret had always known that public hospitals in Hong Kong had reached beyond the saturation point. What she was experiencing in the emergency ward was the norm. Medical staff who didn't quit would have to grit their teeth and get on with their job for as long as their physical and mental strength would allow them. Still, she did not expect the waiting room to be so crowded.

By the time Margaret was done with all the tests and took her first dosage of treatment, it was already seven in the morning. Oddly enough, she didn't feel sleepy. Her mind was still actively running through the events of the last ten hours or so. Not long ago, she was happily eating and drinking with her colleagues, and now, there she was, lying helplessly in a public hospital alongside other patients who had health problems of all sorts. Finally, the medicine took effect. No matter how much she wanted to stay awake, her eyelids became heavy with sleep.

Having slept through pretty much the whole day, Margaret woke up in time to witness the commotion caused by the arrival of a few patients, all of them injured with their eyes and faces bandaged. At first, Margaret didn't pay much attention to these people. As she was about to close her eyes again, she vaguely heard some female voices. Two young women were allocated to the beds next to hers. When their whispers turned into occasional sobs, Margaret became curious and looked their way.

As someone who survived her first day in the hospital, Margaret made an initiative and offered help, "Can I help you? If you need anything, I'll call the nurse for you."

Shaking their heads, they kept looking at something on one of their phones. Margaret observed that they were holding hands all along. During the few moments as they were watching what seemed to be a video clip, they squeezed each other's hands so hard that Margaret could see the veins throbbing under their young, fair skin. Dressed in plain hospital gowns, these two young women wore no makeup. It was a little difficult to tell their ages, but Margaret reckoned that they would be in their late teens or early twenties. Their faces wore no expression other than a sense of helplessness and shock. Assuming that they had just experienced some kind of trauma such as a car accident, Margaret decided to leave them alone. Besides, she started feeling a little hungry now that the medicine had taken effect.

Margaret took the opportunity to ask a nurse who happened to be walking their way whether it would soon be dinner time.

"There is a short delay, but food will be delivered as soon as we are done with some business," said the nurse. Turning to the two women, she said without showing too much expression, "Now, you two must get changed. The police are waiting for you outside."

The two young women appeared shocked and scared. Margaret was also surprised at hearing what the nurse had said. Even though she did not have much experience with crime, she couldn't imagine these two young women were wanted. What would the police arrest the two soft-spoken girls for?

"We are not going anywhere until our parents arrive," said one of the young women.

"I can't do anything. Sorry," said the nurse. "You must do what I told you or I'll get into trouble. Now, get up." The nurse thrust a backpack at each of them. As she was about to walk away, a younger nurse said that they should perhaps let them wait for their parents.

"Mind your own business." The younger nurse who made the suggestion had no choice but to go off with her tail between her legs.

"Oh, please help us," cried the other young woman. "It's not really our fault that the government is so stupid."

"Stop begging her. We'd better do what she told us."

"No! They can't arrest us. We shouldn't be punished for the government's idiotic, wicked actions. Watch this, and you'll understand what I'm saying." The young woman started playing a video clip on her phone, and this time she turned the sound on. She wanted the nurse to watch it, but it was too late, for the nurse had already left the ward.

Seeing that the young woman was still holding her phone in tears, Margaret reached out her hand. "May I?"

Margaret understood everything after she finished watching the video. Even though the image kept shaking, and was at times smoky and blurred, it was clear to Margaret that the two women and those around them were trying to run away from police who were spraying tear gas at the crowds. In the last few months when Margaret was busy dealing with the closure of her company, she almost forgot about the city's anger towards the government's proposal of an extradition law that could make it possible for anyone charged with an offence, the so-called fugitives, to be sent to China for trial. When Hong Kong guaranteed fair and open trials, which is a luxury in China, how could its people not worry about that proposed law? Lawyers, scholars, businesspeople, and professionals of many fields tried to stop the government from passing the law, but it seemed as if those in power had turned blind and deaf.

Now, Kate's insistence that they should all go to a peaceful rally last Sunday came back to her mind. Margaret did not plan to join the march, for life experience had taught her that any attempts at making the government listen to its people were futile. She was doubtful of the outcome, but even so, she went along, since Kate said that it was their last resort. In desperation, people joined together and marched on to the streets. Margaret could tell it was a big turnout, but she didn't expect it to be over a million. What mattered so dearly to these people who took part in the rally was clumsily brushed off by the chief executive, who refused to back down. Margaret couldn't understand what kind of government would take a peaceful rally of over a million people so lightly. Her incomprehension soon turned into worry, then concern for her future.

Similar to what she witnessed in the Umbrella Movement in 2014, this video recording also showed a Harcourt Road with no traffic. A sit-down, peaceful demonstration was now replaced by a direct confrontation: rows of police officers on one side, and thousands of protesters protecting themselves against tear gas and rubber bullets with face masks, goggles, and umbrellas on the other. Whether it was another movement or a continuation of the previous one, Margaret could tell that it had escalated. After she was discharged from the hospital, she learned that to stop the legislative council from passing the law, some young people made a desperate move by blocking all the main roads to the government headquarters. To halt the legislative procedure, they had to bear serious damage to their bodies.

"You stay here," said one of them. "I'll tell the police that you were not involved."

"No, I won't let you do that. Besides, we did nothing wrong; we only wanted to stop the meeting," said her friend. "Remember our promise? Together we start, and together we'll see our revolution to its end. I won't leave you behind."

It wasn't very often that Margaret witnessed a noble act like now. Just when she was figuring how she might help, a team of police officers arrived. Within minutes, all the young people in her ward, including the two young women with whom Margaret had a brief encounter, changed back into their own clothes and were taken away. In the last moment before they walked out, the one who let Margaret watch the video on her phone said, "It's not our fault that we have such a wicked government, is it?"

"No." Margaret paused briefly, for she didn't know what else to say. Her response was as helpless as the one she gave Dominic when he told her that Yang did not love him. How could you comfort someone who experienced a brutal awakening? It was as though Margaret's blessing was important, she added, "Take care," before they disappeared.

It was June 12, 2019, the first week of the extradition bill saga when the hospital staff were caught off guard, thinking that complying with the police order was the right thing to do. In the following days and months, the city experienced more rallies, clashes, confrontations, and even deaths, all of which brought immense sadness and disappointment. People felt ever more helpless and hopeless when the government refused to budge even after two million people took part in another peaceful rally on the following Sunday. On the fourth of September when the chief executive finally announced the official withdrawal of the bill, too much damage had already been done—thousands of people were arrested, at least two young women were hit by police rubber bullets in their eyes, dozens of protesters were brutally beaten up and labelled as rioters, not to mention there were a number of suicides. With blood smeared all over the city, the decision came too late. "The government has no heart. Even if it has one, it must have turned into stone," people lamented. Some felt so desperately hopeless that they even called it a modern version of the Tiananmen Square protests when students went to the front trying to direct the leaders to the right path.

On the hospital bed, Margaret continued to reflect on what happened. Life was unpredictable, that much she knew from her food poisoning experience. In her helpless state, she thought of everyone she knew who had no control over their fate. Kate, for example, was one of the cleverest women she'd ever known. But what was the use of it? When a head hunter approached her with a top job with lucrative perks in the US, she turned it down, saying that she couldn't leave Hong Kong before her brother was released from prison. Margaret tried to change her mind, but she just wouldn't listen. Kate insisted on paying her brother regular visits, saying that the least she could do was to show her moral support. In the beginning, Margaret was mad at Kate for not thinking about her own future, but then she began to see how important it was for Kate to be around. It was her way of reassuring her brother that he did the right thing and that he hadn't been abandoned. Ironically, it was when the body was sick and weak that Margaret could see the matter so much more clearly.

Her experience in the hospital also made her feel awfully trapped, not so much for herself, as she knew that she could get out of there if she chose to. She had enough money to seek medical assistance in a private hospital. But how about the people around her? Or the young people who were arrested by the police? Did they have a choice? Margaret looked at the woman next to her. She finally went to sleep after spending a night wailing in pain. It suddenly occurred to her that the worst thing in life was being trapped as a result of sickness, poverty, or calamities. That had to be how most of the people around her felt.

So, at that moment in the hospital bed, she made up her mind. Unlike before, she did not torment herself with any ifs or buts. She held no ambivalent feelings and acted so fast that her decisiveness surprised everyone. Margaret remembered how Kate reacted to her announcement of leaving Hong Kong.

"What? Are you serious?"

"Yes, I am."

"No, you can't be serious!" Kate exclaimed in disbelief.

"Why not?"

"You love Hong Kong; you can't leave us."

"I can still love the place without being here."

"It won't be the same."

"I don't see the difference."

"The difference is I won't see you. I will miss you a lot." Kate was almost yelling at her.

"Don't worry, we will still see each other, perhaps not as often, but we will," assured Margaret. "In fact, what I have in mind is for you and your brother to move out of Hong Kong one day."

"Why?"

"Why not?" To counter her friend's narrative of pathos, Margaret gave a detailed contrast of two possible futures: one in Canada and another in Hong Kong, using her recent experience at the hospital as the most convincing evidence. She then summarised, "So, if you want clean air, quality water, quality social service—in short, everything that gives you peace of mind—come and live with me in Canada."

"You know my brother won't be able to migrate now that he has a criminal record," said Kate.

"Maybe not for him, we'll see. But you should think about it. You should be thinking about yourself."

They said no more of that for months, until one day Margaret told Kate of her departure. A fixed date urged them to spend more time together. Feeling a sense of urgency, Kate suggested that they should spend a night in the penthouse suite of their favourite hotel again. A night of intimate girl talk Margaret still missed, but as soon as they checked in, she didn't find the place special anymore. The hotel was full of noisy guests, and they occupied every corner in the lobby, the bar, and all the restaurants. Around them were no longer such lovely things as fresh flowers at the reception, piano music in the lobby bar, or a scent of perfume lingering in the female toilet. The good things in life were no longer noticeable with visitors from Mainland China arriving in hordes. In the end, Margaret and Kate resorted to ordering room service.

Margaret wondered if business was so good that the hotel no longer cared to provide quality service anymore. Maybe the hotel hadn't changed, but rather she did. Margaret had become more sophisticated in both her taste and experience over the years. Even the supposedly luxurious room seemed to have shrunk. In order not to spoil the night, Margaret kept those thoughts to herself. They talked a lot, reminiscing about the good old days. They recalled the things they did together, the people they met, and the places they visited. Naturally, their memory took them back to their trip in Beijing and how they argued whether they should go and see Tiananmen Square. Margaret remembered how the sight of the place brought tears to Kate's eyes. Her friend must have been overcome with an emotion that she couldn't relate to at the time. But after she witnessed the Umbrella Movement and the recent protests and saw the same frustration on the faces of the young people in Hong Kong, she began to understand Kate's sentiments.

As she was talking to Kate, she recalled a few lines in her head. Whether it was something Margaret studied in the university or an idea that came in her dream she wasn't sure of, but as her departure drew close, these lines gave her a new meaning: "How we remember the past shapes the present. How politicians record the past determines the future. We must study history and be part of it so we can be in control of our own destiny." It suddenly dawned on her that the journey she was going to make would not be a departure but her homecoming.

A REVELATION

In the years that followed, the two friends lived separately in two countries, far apart from one another, each trying their best to get on with life, adapting to the many changes in their own environment. Margaret was counting in her head the years since she had seen Kate and was trying to decide if she should count the time they met for half an hour at Chek Lap Kok Airport when she was changing flights in Hong Kong.

She started recalling memories from the past soon after she parked her car. Now walking into her favourite bookshop, she heard a familiar greeting, "Hi Margaret, how're you doing today?"

"Oh, hi, Jannah. Didn't expect to see you here. I'm surprised you're working today."

"I've been working every day after Christmas and New Year. Spent too much money."

"I see. I suppose it's still term break."

"That's right," said Jannah. "Might as well make some money before a new term starts."

Jannah worked at least three days a week during term time, and sometimes more because she needed the money. All Margaret knew was Jannah's parents were not rich. In fact, they could hardly afford her tuition fees. Probably because of hardships in life, Jannah seemed more mature than most young people of her age. Margaret enjoyed chatting with her about music, art, literature, philosophy, and sometimes politics. She always gave good recommendations on what to read too. To make sure she was in the shop, Margaret usually called first.

"I missed a call earlier. Was that you?" asked Jannah.

"No, I didn't call today. I wasn't planning to come in, but then I figured that I have a few hours to spare. So, why not buy a few books and read them in the café next door? I like watching the rain and the people walking past."

"Is it still raining?" asked Jannah.

"It was drizzling when I came in."

"Did you say you have a few hours to spare? What's your plan?"

"I'm meeting my friends at the airport. Their flight will arrive in, let me see, seven hours. I haven't seen them for years."

"Wow, that's so cool. Are they staying with you?"

"Yes, of course."

"Pity your friends are coming in a wrong season. It's so cold and wet now."

"Never mind, they'll spend quite some time with me. I am sure we will experience a warmer season later."

"That's good. Now Margaret, if you don't mind, I'll leave you browsing for a while. Give me a minute and I'll be with you. I have to deal with this pile of new arrivals. They just came in this morning." On the counter was a big pile of books of different sizes waiting to be catalogued.

"Sure, I'll leave you to finish your work. I'll take care of myself, don't worry." No sooner had Margaret shown her confidence, than Jannah heard her crying out loudly, "Ouch."

"What's wrong, Margaret? Are you okay?"

Jannah rushed to the back of the shop and saw Margaret kneeling on the floor with books scattered around her.

"I didn't see the pile of books on the floor and walked right into them. Sorry."

"That's okay. I'll pick them up later. Are you okay?"

"Yes, I am fine. I was just trying to save the books from crumpling down onto the floor."

"I should have warned you of these books, but I forgot all about them. They were brought here before Christmas. I think it was a guy who helped to clear stuff from his aunt who had just passed away."

"Oh, really? You mean all these books belonged to the same person?" asked Margaret.

"I think so."

"Can I look at them, or do you need to sort them out first?" Every time Margaret went to see her friends in their home, she always enjoyed looking at their bookshelves to see if they had similar taste of reading materials. Now with someone's life collection of books in front of her, Margaret couldn't resist taking a good look at them.

"Please help yourself. Just let me know if you see anything you like."

As Jannah was piling up the books in several heaps, she was also checking a few that passed her hands. "'Bleak House' by Charles Dickens, 'Collected Poems' by Emily Dickinson. I can't believe it, here's Truman Capote's 'In Cold Blood' and 'Answered Prayers.' Look at that, there are works of translations from other European languages too."

"Jannah, I thought you had work to do."

"It can wait. I want to see this collection first. His aunt had to be someone with good taste."

Margaret was happy to have Jannah sharing this exciting find with her. Together they looked into the piles and started reading a few pages of each book that interested them. Many of these they had already read at some stage of their lives, but when they saw one that they had never heard of before, they read the blurb at the back of the book to decide whether they should put it back into the pile or keep it. Suddenly, it became a wonderful child's game of treasure hunt. A long wait for Kate and her brother's arrival had unexpectedly turned into a new adventure.

Margaret found it hard to keep up with Jannah's reading speed. She nevertheless maintained her own pace and was now picking up one of the books, flipping through the first few pages of a novel by an Estonian writer, Anton Hansen Tammsaare. Jannah was right: the deceased woman had a unique literary taste and a wide range of interests too. Margaret almost felt sorry for not having met this woman in person. The more Margaret tried to imagine what kind of person she once was, the more extraordinary she found the experience. How often would one have the chance to imagine a person's life by examining her books?

"Margaret, see what I found?" Jannah's voice betrayed a sense of astonishment.

"What did you find?"

"It's a collection of poems written by a professor teaching in my university," said Jannah.

"Anything unusual about it?"

"Yes, everything. For one thing, I didn't know he writes literary works, least of all English poetry," said Jannah.

"Why not, if he teaches in the university?"

"You don't understand, Margaret. He's not a typical professor. He is someone who speaks English with a very strong accent. Nobody understands much of his lectures. Students tease him about his accent, sometimes right in his face. I feel really sorry for him."

"Then should he be teaching in the university at all?"

"Now, this is the part you'll find interesting. He is very intelligent and can always come up with a unique perspective on something that everyone thinks is final, done, case closed. Do you see what I mean? What I like most are his power-point slides, which are full of wisdom. He must spend a lot of time preparing them. What he cannot express verbally, he shows to us. It's a shame that my classmates do not see behind the face."

"What do you mean?"

"He is Chinese."

"What's wrong with that? I am Chinese too," protested Margaret.

"But you don't look like one, not at all. I'm talking about someone who lived in China before he came to Canada."

"Oh, I see. What's his research area?"

"History. He's very much into narrative history. He doesn't believe in a grand, single historical narrative that leaders of most nations pass on to the future generations; rather, he takes the view that the study of history is to learn to interpret historical events from different perspectives, including those who are weak and powerless."

"It's so much more meaningful too."

"Yes, isn't it? I never get tired of listening to his stories about the Tiananmen Square." Jannah was interrupted by a customer at the counter who needed her help. "Coming, I'll be right with you." Before she walked back to the front of the shop, Jannah joked with Margaret, "You should read it, since you consider yourself Chinese."

Margaret went to give Jannah a friendly slap but missed. As soon as Jannah started talking to the customer, Margaret recognised the voice. It was one of those who had so much free time and so little to do that it would be a while before her friend would be free to join her again. She decided it would be a good idea to read her professor's collection of poems to pass the time.

On the book cover were a few humble words: *A Collection of Poems by Yang Bun*. No fancy graphics or photos. His name was common and yet unfamiliar. Margaret turned to his bio data, which confirmed what Jannah had already told her. Then, a sentence caught her attention: "Professor Yang continued with his undergraduate studies in Canada in 1989 after he left China." The moment she finished reading the introduction, she felt as if she were talking to this professor in person, except that in her mind's eye, he was much younger, still in his undershirt, looking at her with his shy eyes.

Margaret first read a short poem that he wrote in the millennium, then she turned to the contents page to look for another one that might interest her. *How about this one? The title sounds upbeat and hopeful:* "Oh Joy, Oh Joy! For My Best Friend."

Margaret turned to the page that began with the background of the poem:

> *I started writing this poem in 1997 but couldn't finish it because of an immense sadness and regret. I haven't stopped blaming myself for causing the death of my friend. A deep sense of remorse is still haunting me. I kept forcing myself to look back to the event as a penance. Now, I have a better understanding. Maybe that is life. Maybe my friend had to die so that I can go*

on living. But this doesn't stop me from mocking my luck. Why does my fortune always bring tragedies to people that I love? I survived the killings at the Tiananmen Square, but my comrades did not. I thrive in my career at the expense of my friend's life. I have no explanation for this except that it's our fate. I must accept that I am leading a borrowed life; I gain time from all these tragedies, and I can't help it.

In my weak and trembling voice, I beg you to read the copy of a newspaper report before reading my poem. If you don't read Chinese, you should at least read my friend's last letter. He had a voice with no power. It was a voice of suppressed vitality, a voice of the most ordinary people. I beg you to go on reading.

Margaret read a brief news report about the drowning of a twenty-three-year-old man. His body was found near a ferry pier in Sheung Wan. Even though Margaret was not a proficient reader of the Chinese language, she could tell the report was written in an impersonal, matter-of-fact style. Then she followed Yang's instructions and saw her friend's handwritten letter in print:

Dear Yang,

I know you don't like me writing to you, thinking that I am making all sorts of excuses to get your attention. Let me be straight. It's true that I was once very angry. I even wanted to kill you, but my hatred has disappeared and is now replaced with fear. I fear for you more than for myself. Yes, someone is still following me. Remember I wrote in my last letter saying that I thought it was a mistake? Now I can confirm there is no mistake. I am not paranoid or mad. Someone is really following me. Sometimes there's only one person, but sometimes they come in two or three. I don't know what they want from me. I have no money and no education. So, the only reason I can think of is you. But don't you worry, I will protect you for as long as I can, which is why I write to you in English. It is, of course, silly of me to assume that it is safer to write in English, but somehow I do think so. Also, it's my habit of writing to anyone who lives in Canada in English. I have another friend in Canada, and I write to her only in English.

Again, you probably don't like me reminding you that the eighth anniversary is coming soon, so you can skip this part if you don't want to read it. I am still writing to you because I have to, for my own sake, and for all the student activists who died many years ago. Same as last year and the years before, I will attend the memorial at Victoria Park. This is going to be a very special year—our last gathering under the British flag. I don't know if we can go on with the event next year. I hope we do. Again, I am curious. You don't have to tell me if you don't want to. What do you usually do on the anniversary? Will you light a candle and say a little prayer now that you are a Christian? Will you say your prayer in English or in Chinese? Never mind, you don't have to tell me anything. I am sure you will remember everything without doing anything.

Now that I am reading my letter again, I really like the last few lines. They sound like lyrics. I shall perhaps train myself into a songwriter. That's enough nonsense of me. I should be serious again. Take care. Promise me.

Your most trusted friend,
Dominic
31 May 1997

He did not attend that gathering. He died two days later.

Margaret couldn't hold back her tears anymore. She let them flow with the music in the background. Now, the shop quieted. With no human voices, she could make out Liszt's "Au lac de Wallenstadt." After listening to the first few bars, Margaret gained her calm like the water in the lake and started reading the poem:

Oh Joy, Oh Joy!

Neither sweet nor bitter,
Friendly Hands of Water,
Rising, rising to the Tower.
Neither fright nor sorrow,
Eat your pride, then swallow,
Come alive, tomorrow.
Oh joy, oh joy!

Neither left nor right,
People fight with all their might.
Bloody, bloody, such a sorry sight.
Neither East nor West,
Chanting, praying with hands clasped.
Join them before Heaven opens—Tears dropped.
Oh joy, oh joy!

Neither he nor she
who can tell life is brief.
Deeply buried is our man-made grief.
Neither past nor future,
It's the present moment I treasure.
What a blissful moment of torture.
Oh joy, oh joy!

When Margaret finished reading Yang's poem, her eyes were filled with tears again. First, she felt a deep sadness for Dominic, then a new understanding. She had never accepted that someone who held three jobs would kill himself. It just didn't make sense. This revelation, though sudden, was not a surprise to her. All her doubts about her friend were gone. Dominic was indeed a man with strength. He tried to fight a force much bigger than he but failed. What was he thinking of in his last moments? Was he only trying to remember his love for Yang, or for all student activists too? Was he only dying his own death or that of all things that were once dear to him? To Margaret, Dominic died a martyr to the cause. He truly embodied all the memories that Yang had left behind in a faraway place.

"I am sorry to keep you waiting. I finally got rid of her." On seeing Margaret, Jannah's apology turned into surprise. "Are you okay?"

"Oh yes, it's the music and his poems. I was very touched."

"I told you he's good." Jannah expressed her relief by giving Margaret a hug. "You like the music, don't you? I like it a lot too. Every time I listen to it, I imagine myself looking at this enchanted lake, giving up everything to win its beauty and tranquility:

Thy contrasted lake,
With the wild world I dwelt in, is a thing
Which warns me, with its stillness, to forsake
Earth's troubled waters for a purer spring."

"Oh, it's so beautiful." Margaret's lips quivered, and her tears started again.

"Not my words. Lord Byron's."

"Still, it's good for you to remember them."

"You would too if you studied literature and worked in a bookshop."

"Can I buy his book?" asked Margaret.

"Sure, let me keep it for you. Do you want to continue looking for a while?"

"Probably not. I'll go next door for some coffee before making my way to the airport."

"Sure, let me wrap it up for you."

"No, that's fine. I'll put it in my bag."

After Margaret paid for her book, Jannah said, "Say hello to your friends, and bring them here."

"I will, after they get over jet lag."

"Sure. Take your time. You will have a lot to catch up."

"Yes, a lot. And a lot to think about too. Can we go and visit your professor?"

"Of course. Let me know when your friends are ready. See? I told you my professor is great."

Margaret had to arrange for Kate and her brother to meet Yang. These activists from two generations would have a lot to say to each other. But for now, she simply said, "Yes, we'll go and see him for his autograph."

"No problem, I can help you with that," said Jannah eagerly.

"Thank you. I'll see you later."

"Bye."

As Margaret was leaving the bookshop and walking into the street, it started raining again, but she was in no hurry. She still had a few hours to spare before the long-awaited reunion. She looked up into the sky and wondered, *Do I want to be young again? No, not really. When I was young, I never had much of a feeling for classical music, but now the playing of Bach's preludes and fugues moves me to tears. When I was young, I didn't feel for the poor, but now the sight of poverty brings a lump in my throat. When I was young, I didn't know how to talk to animals, or trees, or bees, or a river, but now the nature and the feeling of existence makes me small and yet full. When I was young, I was too busy trying to convince others of my worth, but now I left my self behind and focus on others' well-being. Why would I want to be youthful and thoughtless again?*

BOOK CLUB QUESTIONS

1. Have you ever joined a protest? If so, why?
2. How hard do you think it would be for you to leave your home the way Margaret left Hong Kong, not once but twice?
3. Do you see Dominic as a strong character the way Margaret concluded he was at the end of the book?
4. Are you satisfied with the way Margaret conducted herself throughout? Why or why not?
5. Why do you think everyone except Margaret accepted that Dominic had killed himself? Is suicide a taboo topic in your culture or in your family?
6. How do you react to the water imagery used in the book?
7. What does the book title mean to you?

Review Requested:

We'd like to know if you enjoyed the book. Please consider leaving a review on the platform from which you purchased the book.

CPSIA information can be obtained
at www.ICGtesting.com
Printed in the USA
LVHW041324310522
720087LV00003B/141

9 781682 356128